**Discover the mystery of Alaska
in this all-new collection of short stories.**

In "Going Home" by **S. J. Rozan**, an Alaskan private investigator tracks down a man's brother in New York City. But does the brother really want to be found?

In **Donna Andrews**'s "An Unkindness of Ravens," nature and myth partner up to put an abusive husband in his place.

In "A Little Walk Home," **Michael Armstrong**'s protagonist triumphs over five hundred miles of Alaskan bush to emerge again into civilization.

In "The Twin" by **Brad Reynolds**, Native Alaskan culture steps in when a ceremonial mask comes to life.

**Plus eight more chilling tales of the
great mysterious North!**

THE
MYSTERIOUS
NORTH

Tales of Suspense from Alaska

Edited by
Dana Stabenow

A SIGNET BOOK

SIGNET
Published by New American Library, a division of
Penguin Putnam Inc., 375 Hudson Street,
New York, New York 10014, U.S.A.
Penguin Books Ltd, 80 Strand,
London WC2R 0RL, England
Penguin Books Australia Ltd, Ringwood,
Victoria, Australia
Penguin Books Canada Ltd, 10 Alcorn Avenue,
Toronto, Ontario, Canada M4V 3B2
Penguin Books (N.Z.) Ltd, 182–190 Wairau Road,
Auckland 10, New Zealand

Penguin Books Ltd, Registered Offices:
Harmondsworth, Middlesex, England

First published by Signet, an imprint of New American Library,
a division of Penguin Putnam Inc.

First Printing, October 2002
10 9 8 7 6 5 4 3 2 1

Contents

Introduction

What is it about Alaska that, when I'm on a book tour Outside and tell people I'm from here, their eyes kind of go out of focus and they breathe, "Alaska," in a voice just this side of reverent? Actually, it's more like "Ah-laaaaaas-kah," a long, drawn-out exhalation that embodies a longing as strong as it is inarticulate.

A longing for what, exactly?

We've always been a wandering race. We wandered out of Africa into Europe and Asia, across the Pacific and the Bering land bridge into North and South America. It's no different today. When we're kids, it's the other side of the fence. When we're teenagers, it's the next town and maybe even the next state, anything to get away from our parents. When we're adults and have assumed adult responsibilities like jobs, marriage, and children, it's the lure of the frontier—a place that is as wide open geographically as it is socially and culturally—that beckons us, a chance to start over, to remake ourselves, if only for a two-week vacation.

The difference today is that there are pitifully few wide-open places left for us to go.

Alaska is such a place. Yes, we have cable television and cell phones and, in the cities, at least, flush toilets, but for most Alaskans their personal history stops at the Beaver Creek border crossing or at the gate at SeaTac and starts all over again this side of the border.

Here are just a few of the things that make us different.

Take physical size. Alaska is one-fifth the size of the rest of the United States, and twice the size of the next biggest state, Texas. Lay a map of Alaska over the South 48 and it will overlap both borders and both coasts. I was born here fifty years ago and I haven't seen half of it.

Which brings us to transportation, which brings us to planes. One of every fifty-eight Alaskans has a pilot's license. Some of them don't bother with driver's licenses. Why? Because there are few roads, a little over 14,000 miles' worth and only 22 percent of them paved, and because much of the shoreline (36,000 miles of it) freezes up during winter, restricting boat access. If you want to get anywhere, you fly, in anything from a Piper Super Cub to a de Havilland Beaver to a DC-3 to a Boeing 737. It's basic transportation, the Alaskan equivalent of the New York subway system.

We eat and dress a little differently, too. Rural Alaskans wear fur as a matter of survival. Rural Alaskans hunt as a matter of subsistence. Go ahead, throw a bucket of red paint on someone wearing a fur parka. Do me a favor first, okay? Warn me, so I can dive out of the way of the bullets.

Which brings me to firearms. Michael Armstrong tells a great story about arriving in Barrow to work on an archaeological dig, and one of the first sounds he hears is of an automatic rifle going off in the distance. A firearm in the Alaskan Bush is a tool, not a toy. Pretty much everyone wears or carries a knife, too—Swiss Army or Leatherman—and on intrastate flights most air taxis don't make you check them. If the plane goes down, it's your primary piece of survival gear.

About food. There is a story, probably apocryphal but no less true for that, about a vegetarian who moved to the Bush and starved to death in a month. Bush rats are for the most part card-carrying omnivores, with reason. Surviving Alaskan winters means eating anything that a) doesn't eat you first, and b) doesn't get out of the way fast enough. When I was a kid, it was simple: If we didn't get a moose that fall, we didn't eat meat that winter.

And then there is our history. It didn't start with statehood all the way back in 1959, oh no. Seven different major tribes of Alaska Natives—Tlingits and Haida and Tsimshian in Southeast, Aleut in Southcentral and Southwest, Yupiq in the West, Inupiaq in the North, and Athabascan in the Interior—and the anthropologists are still arguing over who came from where and when. Captain Cook sailed into what was later named Cook Inlet in his honor in 1778, and

Turnagain Arm is called so because instead of discovering the Northwest Passage, he had to turn
again. The last shot in the Civil War was fired by the
Confederate warship *Shenandoah* in the South's effort
to disrupt the North's economy by sinking Yankee
whalers. The only United States territory to be occupied by the Japanese during World War II was in
Alaska, Attu and Kiska Islands. Never mind the
Klondike Gold Rush and the oil discoveries at
Prudhoe Bay.

The amount of weight you carry in the state is
directly proportional to how long you've been here.
Alaska Natives win hands down here, followed by
the folks descended from Russian *promishliniki*, Scan-
dinavian whalers, Army surveyors, Klondike stampeders, Seattle fishermen, Midwest homesteaders,
American GI's, and Nikiski roughnecks. Or any combination thereof.

So when I asked a group of writers to contribute
a story for an anthology of fiction set in Alaska, I
knew enough to know I had no idea what was coming. And I was right.

We've got stories from all over the Alaska map,
Mike and Sue's in Anchorage, albeit sixty years apart,
Kate's also from Anchorage, Anne's from Seward,
Kim's in Fairbanks, Jim's in Northwest, Brad's in
Southwest, Donna's in Ketchikan,' Michael's in the
Interior, mine in the Chilkoot Pass, and S.J.'s isn't
even in Alaska at all.

We've got stories from all over the timeline, mine
in the Klondike Gold Rush, Mike's in World War II
and featuring no less than Dashiell Hammett, Anne's

in 1964, Kim's in 1975, and the rest in the present day.

We've got stories from every walk of Alaskan life, Bush to city dweller, and then Donna and Kate throw us curveballs by giving us the tourist's-eye view.

Alaska itself, myth and reality both, is an integral part of each of the stories, one could even say a character. In Anne's aptly titled "Rearrangements," three sisters contend with each other even as they contend with the Good Friday Earthquake of 1964. In Donna's "An Unkindness of Ravens," nature and myth partner up to take an abusive husband in hand. In Kim's "Terminal," construction on the 800-mile-long Trans-Alaska Pipeline doesn't stop even for murder. In "A Little Walk Home," Michael's protagonist triumphs over 500 miles of Alaskan Bush to emerge again into civilization.

In Brad's "The Twin," Native culture steps in when a Yupiq mask comes to life. In Jim's "The Word for Breaking August Sky," the heavens themselves open up to the story's characters. In John's narrative poem, "Finding Lou," an Alaskan detective's own nature gets in his way when he's looking for a fisherman who might have killed an old man. Or might not.

Myself, I set my story in the Gold Rush, because I hiked the Chilkoot Trail in 2000 and I still can't get over how many times the stampeders had to climb the pass to hump their supplies into Canada. Seventy feet of snow fell on the Chilkoot Pass that winter. I still don't know how the Lion of the Yukon, Samuel Benton Steele of the Royal Canadian Mounted Police, managed to keep the peace. Not to stain his character, but just supposing he didn't . . .

The writers themselves are a mixed bag, some from Alaska, some not, some setting foot here for the first time in 2001 because I coerced them into attending the Left Coast Crime convention in February. Anne Perry came all the way from Scotland, S. J. Rozan from New York City, Donna Andrews from Virginia, and Kate Grilley from the Caribbean. Some of us are homegrown—Kim Rich and Mike Doogan and me. Some of us are transplants who took—Michael Armstrong and Sue Henry and John Straley and Jim Sarafin. Brad's a Jesuit priest who served in Bush Alaska for many years.

So here, for your reading pleasure, eleven stories and one poem, all set in Alaska. It is an extreme landscape, three mountain ranges, thousands of streams, creeks and rivers, rolling tundra that stretches on for hundreds of miles.

Such an extreme landscape inevitably breeds extreme personalities. You put four Alaskans in a room, you'll have five marriages, six divorces and seven political parties.

You may also have . . . murder.

Enjoy.

—Dana Stabenow

AN UNKINDNESS OF RAVENS
Donna Andrews

"You don't mind if Emmy tags along with you in Ketchikan, do you?"

I smoothed away my frown before Emma could see it.

"Of course not, Tom."

It wasn't a lie; I liked Emma. We'd spent a lot of time together since our Alaskan cruise began six days ago. Most of the passengers, from the thirtysome-things like Tom and Emma to the senior citizens like me, launched themselves off the boat at each stop as if competing to see who could squeeze in the most hiking, kayaking, sightseeing, and shopping before the inevitable evening departure.

Emma and I called ourselves the cane gang.

Hers was metal, well-worn, and practical, legacy of an auto accident that had permanently damaged her left leg. Mine was newer and more fanciful; I'd chosen the carved wooden falcon's head with an eye to its other uses, after I got over my hip replacement surgery and could walk unaided. "Think how decorative it will look in my hall umbrella stand," I told friends who called it impractical. No, I didn't mind Emma. I minded Tom using me to get Emma out of the way so he could pursue his latest affair without interference.

Not that Emma seemed to mind. Or even notice.

"I feel so much safer, knowing there's someone with me to call for help if I fall," I said.

Tom hooted with laughter.

"You hear that, Emmy?" he said. "You might even be useful for a change!"

I flinched. Not Emma. She accepted his perfunctory kiss on the cheek and watched with her usual steady, untroubled face as Tom, still laughing, trotted down the gangplank, talked with other disembarking passengers, and eventually left in a group that, as always, contained a certain lively redheaded divorcée. I knew Emma would sip her tea and wait, patiently, until I was ready. Whatever agenda I had in mind was always exactly what she wanted to do, and as soon as I noticed that my hip was beginning to ache, I'd hear her apologetic suggestion that perhaps we might sit down somewhere for a time, or perhaps head back to the ship.

The perfect companion, at least for something as sedate as this cruise. And I had to admit that my hip wasn't ready for the kind of energetic outdoor excursions I usually favored. Pretending I was slowing down for Emma helped make our pace tolerable. And yet I had the curious feeling that left to her own devices, she'd sit all day on the deck, feeding the seagulls.

Or reading one of the books she'd always stuff into her purse when I came to the table—books on Tarot, astrology, and every other kind of mysticism.

I suspected that Tom's arrangements to keep her out of the way often saddled her with less congenial companions. And that, on their frequent travels, Emma spent a great deal of time enduring the company of strangers.

I was pleasantly surprised when she seemed excited about Ketchikan.

"You'll like it," she said, several times, peering through the window. "It's really quite beautiful. The way the houses cling to the side of the hill. And you'll love Creek Street, where they've reconstructed a few blocks to show what the town looked like in frontier days. And everywhere you look, you can see ravens and eagles—"

"You've seen pictures, then?" I asked.

"Oh, I've been here before," she said. "I—we stayed here for a week, two years ago. I made friends here. It was really quite magical."

I scrubbed the condensation from a patch of window and peered out, trying to catch a glimpse of the magic for myself. But all I could see were sheets of rain. And the occasional raven wheeling outside. Perhaps they were used to being drenched. Well, it made a change, at least, the black ravens instead of the usual seagulls. I wasn't particularly keen on going out in the downpour, but the sight of Emma actually eager for something touched me.

"Just let me go to the cabin for my rain gear," I said.

But I didn't much need my boots and slicker, as it turned out. A minute or two before we walked down the gangplank, the rain stopped, and by the time we had gone a few blocks, the sun began breaking through the clouds.

She was right; I did love the reconstructed Creek Street area. It lay on the banks of a small creek that emptied into the harbor. And since Ketchikan had extreme tides—a difference of as much as thirty feet between high and low tide at the equinox—all the old-fashioned buildings perched on tall wharves and pilings. A wide, weathered boardwalk ran down one side of the creek, then crossed and ran back the other. Occasionally, the walk branched off into alleys, or stairways that angled back and forth across the steep hillside until they reached the top of the cliff. I could see other boardwalks circling the hill at higher levels, and felt a brief pang of regret. Before my surgery, I'd gladly have spent hours climbing up and down the stairs and exploring the walkways on the hillside.

"It's all right," Emma said. "You can come back again, when your hip is better. Anyway, it's pretty slippery up there after it rains."

I started, then realized that perhaps it didn't take a mind reader to guess my thoughts as I stared up at the hillside. I sighed, then frowned at my beautiful falcon cane.

And there was plenty to explore at ground level. We strolled up and down the boardwalk, wandering into a shop occasionally, and spending long stretches of time leaning on the railing, watching the creek and the harbor. Emma, of course, fed the birds—not only the perennial seagulls but also the enormous sleek ravens that seemed to follow us everywhere, their bright stares oddly suggestive of unbirdlike intelligence.

"Do you know what a group of ravens is called?" Emma asked. "An unkindness of ravens. Isn't that funny? They're so clever; I'm sure they must be among the kindest of birds."

I found myself wondering, curiously, if Emma really knew people in Ketchikan. "I made friends here," she'd said. But so far we hadn't met any, and it was a small place.

Or perhaps we did meet them, everywhere. The nonsense Emma cooed as she fed the birds was starting to sound almost sensible. For that matter, I found myself thinking, absently, that with a little study, I might understand what the ravens croaked back.

Eventually, we hooked up with a group from the ship who'd found a guide and were taking a tour of the Creek Street area. A senior citizen's group, so Emma and I didn't have too much trouble keeping up.

"Dolly's is the only original structure on Creek Street," our guide said, pointing to a white Victorian frame house along the wide-board sidewalk. "All the rest have been reconstructed. Of course, it's appropriate that Dolly's survived, since it was one of the most famous fancy houses."

"One of them?" a tourist said. "There were more?"

"Oh, yes," the guide exclaimed. "Creek Street was the red-light district in those days. Half the buildings were brothels, then."

We all studied Dolly's, implausibly demure and cheerful for a brothel.

"Small town to have such a big red-light district," one tourist remarked.

"Ah, but Ketchikan was a major port of call for the fishing fleets that traveled up from the lower forty-eight. And gold miners, coming to town to celebrate their strikes."

I glanced up and down Creek Street, trying to imagine its bawdy heyday by superimposing movie-born images of Storyville and Gold Rush San Francisco on the scene in front of me and failing, miserably. Everything seemed so wholesome. On the other side of the creek, some boys were jumping into the water, trying to land with a maximum of noise and splashing. Upstream, ducks and seagulls swam among the pilings, only a little way below the railings, since the tide was high. They gathered quickly whenever a pedestrian paused to lean over the railing and stare down at the water.

"Of course, it wasn't just the miners and fishermen who visited Dolly's and the other houses," our guide said. "See that path that comes down from the top of the hill?"

We glanced up to see another of the boardwalks, hugging the hillside, then, as the slope grew steeper, descending rapidly through several twisting flights of steps until it finally joined the main Creek Street walk a block or so away.

"That's the Married Men's Path," our guide said. "Single men came through the front door, of course;

but respectable married men would sneak down that path and through the back door to Dolly's."

I couldn't help glancing at Emma. She appeared not to be listening. She was staring out over the water with a half smile on her face. Watching the ducks, gulls, and ravens. Or pretending to watch.

How did those respectable Victorian wives feel about Dolly's, I wondered? Did any of them put up a fuss when their straying husbands slunk home, bright-eyed with guilt and drink? Or did they smile and practice the same deliberate ignorance? Or was the ignorance genuine?

Not with Emma, anyway. As our guide gathered us up and shooed us on to the next stop, I saw Emma glance at Dolly's, a short, sharp glance, full of pain and hatred. And then the usual mask descended; the half smile returned, and she followed our guide's instructions to look toward the harbor.

She knew, I decided. About the Married Men's Path, in all its modern incarnations.

The tour ended at the foot of a small cable car, which carried pedestrians from the boardwalk up to the hotel and restaurant on the top of the hill. Most of the party went up for a midafternoon tea break, but Emma and I headed back to the ship for a rest.

"I wouldn't mind staying here longer," I said, when we reached the dock. But I knew that by the time I had recovered from our afternoon's exertions, the ship would be pulling out, and we'd be heading for our next port of call. Emma and I leaned over the ship's railing, looking back at the town.

I was tired and, I'll admit it, a little cranky. My hip ached, my back ached, my temples throbbed, and I was beginning to realize that my friends had been right—my wonderful walking stick was a little impractical. The handle wasn't the right shape for my hand; it had rubbed my palm raw in several places. And I was tired of the way the ship's itinerary dragged me away every time I started to know and like a town. Emma was right; I should come back to Ketchikan when I was better.

Laughter interrupted my thoughts. Tom's braying laugh, and a high, whinnying giggle from the redhead. I saw them, coming up the gangplank together, obviously sharing a joke. I glanced at Emma, who gazed out across the water, imperturbable.

I felt a brief, fierce flash of anger at Tom; a sudden wish to see him punished; humiliated, hurt, even dead—and I started as the wooden bird writhed in my hand.

"Is something wrong?"

I was staring at my stick. Which didn't appear to have changed at all. Only my imagination. I must have tightened my hand in anger. Perhaps even had a muscle spasm; I certainly was exhausted enough.

"I'm just tired," I said, looking back at Emma. "Tired, and perhaps a little light-headed. I need that nap."

Emma, nodded, and turned back to the railing. She didn't seem terribly upset that our day in her beloved Ketchikan was over. I left her standing on deck, looking up at the birds wheeling overhead. Some of the ravens had followed us back to the ship and were crowding out the gulls as Emma reached into her carryall and pulled out a box of crackers. Back in my cabin, I studied the cane. It didn't seem to have changed. And yet it had. It no longer chafed my hand. It felt as easy and comfortable as the hand itself. You're becoming dotty in your old age, I told myself, dropping off to sleep. Talking ravens. Wooden falcons changing shape.

To my surprise, when I woke from my nap, the ship's engines were still quiet. In the lounge, I heard that the ship had a minor mechanical problem. We'd be staying in Ketchikan until a part could be flown up from Seattle. At least overnight.

"Come on!" Emma said, almost dancing up to me, despite her cane. "We're going to eat in the restaurant on the top of the hill. It's magical, looking down on the lights of the town and the harbor."

My enthusiasm for dining on shore shrank when I realized we would be part of a large, noisy party. But by that time, I was stuck. The restaurant was quite good, but there were too many people, talking too loudly, drinking too much, laughing at Tom's increasingly cruel jokes.

I drank too much myself, far exceeding the modest nightly glass of wine the doctor allowed me while I was still on the painkillers. And instead of damping my irritation, the wine only fed it, until I felt a sharp stab of pain go through my head each time I heard Tom's overly hearty voice or the redhead's shrill giggle.

Emma didn't seem much bothered—I supposed she was used to this kind of party—but as soon as I finished my meal, I said goodnight, pleading a headache.

"I'll go along; you don't want to be walking around alone, even here," Emma said.

"Good idea, Emmy," Tom said, patting her arm carelessly. "This way we won't spoil everyone's fun, having to haul you back to the ship when the party's just getting started."

Emma and I rode the tram down in silence, but when we reached Creek Street, as if by some silent agreement, instead of heading back to the ship we turned in the other direction, and strolled up and down the boardwalk in a drizzle so light it was almost a mist, stopping every now and then to gaze over the water. The moon was full, turning the harbor to silver, but the tide was low, reducing the creek to a few small, sluggish channels.

Probably a good thing to walk off some of the wine before going to bed, I thought. And I was starting to feel better.

Until I heard a familiar voice. A familiar laugh, softer, but still raucous.

Or was I imagining it? Emma didn't react. I left her leaning on the railing and strolled a little farther along the boardwalk, toward the voice, but slowly, as if merely wandering. I turned a corner and realized that I was at the foot of the Married Men's Path. Glancing up, I saw Tom and the redhead on one of the stair landings, embracing. Then they drew apart and began descending the next to last flight of stairs.

Damn the man, I thought. I needed to get Emma away.

I turned back, walking as quickly and quietly as I could, feeling the pressure of those footsteps above and behind me.

And then I heard voices ahead. A man's voice and a woman's. Soft, conspiratorial. At least, they seemed to be ahead of me. Had I miscalculated where the Married Men's Path joined the walkway? No. I glanced back and saw Tom and the redhead, where I expected them to be. He was sitting on the railing, lighting a cigarette. She was talking away from me, giggling and waving as she retraced her way up the stairs. Perhaps the water had somehow amplified their voices while disguising their direction.

Or had someone joined Emma?

"Emma?" I called, softly.

"Over here."

She was still standing where I'd left her, by the railing in the shadow of a building. There was no one with her. Only a raven, perched nearby, watching attentively, as if expecting to be fed.

As I approached, the raven took wing and flew off down the creek, into the deeper shadows.

"We should go back to the ship," I said. I didn't want Emma to see Tom and the redhead. Never mind how good she was at pretending not to be hurt.

Then I heard a startled cry, followed by a splash. A distant splash, from back along the boardwalk, where the shadows were deepest. Distant, but quite distinct. Not the full, exuberant, rolling splash of the children jumping in at high tide, but the small, staccato splash of something falling from the board-walk and hitting a few inches of water over the solid mud and rock of the creekbed. Something . . . or someone.

And I knew in a few seconds we'd begin to hear the aftermath. A shout, or perhaps a scream. Hurried footsteps on the boards. Someone would give the alarm; a siren would approach from the distance. Someone would spot us and word would spread. People from the ship would begin to hover nearby, waiting, with an all-too-human mixture of pity and morbid curiosity, to see the moment when a wife learned that she was now a widow.

Emma, of course, would carry it off beautifully. Almost overcome with grief, yet holding it together bravely. With the help of her devoted friend. I gripped my cane and turned. Time to take my place at her side, ready to play my role.

A raven had landed on the railing near us, and Emma was cooing softly to it, offering it a cracker. As I watched, the raven sidled closer and took the cracker from her hand, then lingered for a few moments as she slowly extended a finger and scratched the side of his head. She turned and smiled at me, brushing a few cracker crumbs from the front of her sweater.

I heard the expected scream from the shadows. Emma leaned against the railing, staring out toward the harbor, her back toward the creek.

As I joined her, the raven flew away. I heard the rustle of his wings as he flew into the shadow, and then the rustle swelled, and he was joined by hundreds of his kind.

A LITTLE WALK HOME
Michael Armstrong

On the evening that Tom Foster walked out of the
wilderness, the sun finally came out after a week of
clouds and fog. A high-pressure front moved in from
the west, and as the sun set, it emerged into clear
sky, bathing the plain below in that glorious red
glow seen only in late summer and early fall. Two
weeks of hard frost had turned berry bushes red, and
alders and willows pale yellow. The gray of the bark
on the bushes blazed silver in the low light shining
on either side of the creek. Up in the hills the kin-
nikinnik and crowberry bushes had turned to purple.

Tom slipped off his pack and watched the sunset,
debating whether to move on or camp on the flat
ground above the creek. His dog, Zydeco, stood next
to him. Tom patted the big husky's thick ruff. In
such moments he forgot that he had been lost in the
wilderness for an entire winter, a whole year, that he
and Zy had wasted away to hard muscle and the

memory of fat. He had lost himself in the wilderness, in the pureness of the land and the glory of nature.

When the eighteen-wheeler kicked up the dust like a comet skimming the ground, Tom had to think, had to reorganize neural connections, so that he saw the truck and the dust long before he remembered what it meant. And then he did. The low rumble of the truck's diesel engine, of its tires rolling over gravel, shocked him into realization, a third sensory impression—truck, dust, diesel—causing his neurons to triangulate.

Truck. Road. Rescue.

Tom pulled out his Cassull .454, sighted through the scope and saw the truck. The sun moved down a notch, light catching on shiny steel, blinking back at Tom. He looked closer and saw more steel, a snake of steel zigzagging next to the road. The Haul Road. The Alaska Pipeline.

He had made it.

Tom smiled, then grinned. He wanted to break into a little jig, leap up and down, hug Zy. He thought, It's an easy hour's hike to the Pipeline corridor and the road. Hell, after a solid month of hiking, hiking as long as he could stand it because at least it kept him warm, one hour would be nothing. The sun would set before he got to the road, though, and as much as he wanted to continue on, he owed the wilderness one last night. Besides, he had found a good place to camp.

"Let's settle in," he said to Zydeco.

Tom put the long-barreled revolver in its holster, thought of the two bullets still chambered in it. He had told himself that if it came to it and Zy lay down to die, he'd end his misery with one of the bullets. The other he'd saved for himself, in case he'd given up somewhere between the Haul Road and the cabin up there in the Brooks Range he had left five hundred miles ago. Might not need those bullets after all.

He opened the backpack, took out the last of his meat, the dried pemmican he had kept as a reserve. For the past two weeks he'd lived on rabbits and voles, and once the picked-over bones of a winter-kill moose.

On a bare patch of gravel along the creekbed, raw and exposed by spring floods, he set up his fire equipment. He didn't like to make but one fire a day. This close to the road, he thought he could dip into his last cache of matches—matches not to make a cooking fire easier, but to start a signal fire fast if he needed it. He'd been in the loneliest damn place in Alaska and it turned out there had never been hope of a stray plane passing by. Tom got one last fire going, one last cooking fire started. While it heated up, he went to the creek and filled up his water pot.

The creek had almost closed up. That had been one of Tom's worries hiking out. He didn't know exactly when freeze-up would hit, or if he would come to some stream he would have to cross, only to find it fast and flowing from fall storms, or worse, jammed with ice and slush too unsafe to cross.

He had delayed leaving the safety of the cabin until mid-fall, when the ground had nearly frozen solid but the heavy snows not yet come. When there would be some snow on the ground, but not cold enough that he would need twice as much food to stay warm. He couldn't always count on finding dry wood to burn, not along the creeks and not in the taiga, the stunted spruce forests of the southern Brooks Range foothills. And he had to hope for some open water so as to save fuel.

The whole walk out had been like that, shooting for an open window of time where he wouldn't run out of food, fuel, weather or any of the other dozen factors that would make walking five hundred miles in mid-fall across wilderness totally impossible. Doing it with a dog, a companion, had added to the risk, but as Tom got a pot of water going and prepared Zy a meal, he thought again how he had justified it: Zy could hunt, too, and if it came to it, he could eat the dog, and he wouldn't need to have hauled the meat until the end.

After he'd made a simple broth of marrow cakes and some scraps of moose jerky for himself and Zy, Tom sat staring at that pipeline glinting in the setting sun. Home at last. He wondered what he would find at home, if Jackie would still be alive and what had happened to his buddy Frank, and why they had abandoned him.

That question had obsessed him since the previous fall, six weeks after Frank had dropped him off at the little lake and the lake had frozen up. It had been Frank who offered the cabin, offered to fly Tom out there. Frank had been the only other guy at the brokerage with the guts to take a grubstake and risk day trading. They'd watched each other's fortunes rise and fall, fall and rise, finally stabilizing at twenty times what they had put in. In the process, the way foxhole buddies grow closer, he and Frank had become the best of friends, the kind who would do anything for each other. So when things turned sour in Tom's marriage too, it had been Frank who suggested Tom get away from it all, work out some problems not just in the marriage—but also in his life. Frank had this little cabin out there in the Brooks, on an old mining claim he'd inherited from his uncle, and did Tom want to go out there and think things through? It had sounded like a good idea at the time, Tom remembered.

Tom looked at that Pipeline, thought of it leading all the way south to Valdez, thought of the roads it crossed that would lead him to Fairbanks, to the home in the hills above the city. He thought of the warmth and security of a home connected by roads to a city, and how he would never, ever take that for granted.

Not after the wilderness.

Four weeks of bliss, two weeks of terror, four months of mind-numbing boredom, then a summer to recover and hope for rescue. In his worst moments he thought of that first month alone over a year ago, a guy and his dog, in a cabin in late summer and early fall. Tom remembered how the alders and birches seemed to turn yellow overnight, how the snow would crawl down the sides of the mountains not steadily, but in quick bursts of storm. When the land around the cabin turned hard, and the underbrush turned six shades of red and purple, he felt his worries soften. At first he babbled incessantly to Zy, so hungry for conversation he sought it in a dog, only Zy hardly talked back, not even barks or woofs, just an occasional yip or a soft growl.

So absorbed had he become in the land, Tom remembered, that he didn't even realize when the plane had failed to come. One day he glanced down at his watch and saw the date, then checked his day planner and realized Frank should have flown in two days before. Well, the lake had been socked in, the high pass leading out of it clouded in mist, so he figured Frank hadn't dared come up the box canyon. Overshoot the lake a few miles and there wouldn't be enough room for even a Super Cub on floats to turn around. A good pilot didn't take chances like that, and you didn't get a pilot better than Frank.

Days turned into weeks, the lake iced up and Tom realized Frank wouldn't be coming. By then he had used up almost all his food, down to maybe five days if he stretched it, and he came to understand that he had been somehow abandoned or forgotten.

A steady *thuck-thuck* broke him out of his reverie. Helicopter, he realized. Okay, he thought, that would be Alyeska security, doing a patrol of the Pipeline route. Good, right? Then he thought, no, as much as it would save him a walk to have Alyeska spot his fire and pick him up, he didn't want that. Too many questions to answer right then, Tom thought. Too much to explain. He would make his appearance in the world in his own time, his own way—on his own terms.

Tom kicked the logs into the snow and then threw handfuls of snow on top of the coals. The steam rose up in a big cloud, quickly dissipating. He watched the helo fly by on the other side of the Pipeline, heading south, probably the last run of the day.

He hauled out his sleeping bag, laid the cracked and patched Ensolite pad out on the ground on top of a tattered tarp, rolled out the bag and crawled into it. Zy curled up next to him, nose tucked into belly, and as he did every night when he went to sleep, Tom wondered if he got more heat from his dog, or Zy from him.

He woke up to one of those glorious days that made him realize why he lived in Alaska despite the hard winters, despite the hard winter he had just gone through, the worst imaginable. Months of below-zero weather could be made tolerable—barely—by a midfall morning. The prospect of another winter could be made bearable by one last grasp of sunny weather, weather not quite cold enough that you could believe winter might never come, that the warmth of a higher sun still surprised you.

Tom went down to the creek to get water and gather wood for one last fire. As he worked, he thought how two weeks ago he began to believe he might just make it out, when he had turned the corner from fatalism to hope. The growing cold compelled him to keep going, to escape the damn wilderness. As the earth nodded off into its long slumber, he came alive. He kept moving west, and while he could only guess how far he moved in a day, he had to believe that eventually he would go so far west he would find that road. And he had.

Today, he thought, today would be the day he could allow himself to come back to life. He walked back up to his camp and got a fire going and a pot of water boiling. The sun and the fire warmed him. He felt his body grow light the same way he had felt when he first fell in love—not the crazed, hormone-driven love of adolescence, but a longer love, what he felt when he realized he wanted to live the rest of his life with Jackie.

Jackie had been one of those women not quite grown into her beauty in high school: tall and gawky, with a nose too big, lips too full, eyes too deep in their knowing. She'd had this great hair, though, light brown with blond glints that bleached out in the summer. He'd been afraid of her steadfast confidence and her intelligence, smart like him, smarter than him, even. When they wound up at the same college, in some of the same classes, either she came to notice him or he grew less afraid, and somehow they fell in love.

Tom fed Zy some warm broth and the last of their food. He nibbled on a bit of moose jerky, but was so excited he hardly had any appetite. He took out an old washcloth and tattered towel, his last bit of soap, stripped off his shirt and washed. If he got lucky, a trucker would pick him up. No need to make the guy suffer from his stench. Tom washed his beard and hair and tried to comb it into something present-able. Looking at himself in the mirror of his Silva compass, he shook his head. He'd tried to keep his hair trimmed neatly, but there was only so much you could do with the little scissors on a Swiss Army knife.

Tom rose and packed, packed for the last time in the wilderness. He thought of leaving behind things he'd carried so long and wouldn't need again: the battered aluminum water pot, the ratty ground tarp, the plastic water bottle he used as a piss pot so he wouldn't have to get out of his sleeping bag on cold nights. To leave the metal and plastic there, though, would be to mar the land, and he couldn't do that, not after the land had made it possible for him to pull through.

The Haul Road beckoned, and Tom walked toward civilization.

All through that hard winter he had debated whether he should try to hike out in the early spring or wait until summer. Frank had lent Tom the Cassull .454 long-barreled revolver with a scope, a light firearm for bear protection and survival hunting, and given him a box of rounds. Tom would rather have had a good rifle, but months later he appreciated the light weight of the handgun, how it didn't hang up in heavy brush, how it allowed him to move through willow and come up close on moose for a sure and single-shot kill.

He'd bagged two moose, one in the fall, nice and fat, one in the winter, scrawny and near death, and they had made all the difference. It gave him the energy to last until spring, until he got two black

bears coming up on the bait station he'd set up from
the moose bones. Those gave him the energy to last
into summer, when the lake opened up and he
thought maybe a plane would be likely to come
find him.

Tom had tried to figure out why Frank had abandoned him, why Jackie hadn't told anyone of his absence, why there hadn't been a search. Surely they
both knew he had gone off to Frank's cabin. Then he
figured it out: They had both been killed in some
accident—Frank was a terrible driver—before they
could alert anyone of his absence. The secret of where
he had gone had died with them. That had to have
been what happened.

Well, he thought, maybe Frank's kids or his ex-
wife would come up and settle the estate, think to
check out the old cabin, and come up that summer
and find Tom. Yeah, that would be how he'd be rescued. Only no one had come last spring, when the
lakes opened up, or last summer, or in early fall.
About six weeks ago Tom had made his decision. He
would not spend one more winter in that cabin waiting for rescue. He would build up his strength, hunt
as much as he could carry and he and Zy would
walk out. They would make their own damn rescue.

When Tom came up to the Haul Road, officially the
Dalton Highway, the sudden artificiality of it stunned
him. It slashed through the willow scrub and tundra
like the claw of a colossus. He pushed on the road
with his foot, felt the packed gravel, picked at the

filter fabric eroding out of the shoulder. The morning sun had melted ice, turning the road to mud, and the tracks of a semi cut through the mud crisp and clear. Tom grinned as if he'd seen fresh moose tracks on a river sandbar.

He hadn't quite thought what he would do, where he would go once he found the Haul Road. For weeks he had dreamed of it, a river of technology, the road that supplied the oil fields to the north, that brought back the trash and junk cast off by the fields on the deadhaul. All he knew was that when he reached it, it would only be a matter of time until he was saved.

So when off in the distance he heard the rumble of a semi driver shifting his rig's gears, when he saw Zy's ears prick up, when he saw a cloud of dust rise from behind a hill just to the north and then the truck came over the hill, for a moment Tom didn't quite know what to do, and then he did what anyone would do in his situation: He raised his thumb, and waved as the truck went by.

The driver went on for a bit, which didn't bother Tom any; there would be other trucks. He started to turn and then saw the truck's brake lights blink on, emergency flashers following, and the truck slowing in a hurricane of dust. Tom put on his pack and ran toward the truck.

When he got there, the driver had stepped out of the truck, and stood by the passenger's side on the shoulder, hands on hips. The guy had a little Glock jammed into his belt, but stared at Tom with more wonder than malice. Tom kept his hands away from the Cassull—no need to get shot in self-defense in the process of being rescued.

"Man, you look like shit warmed over," the truck driver said to him. "Where the hell did you come from?"

Tom caught his breath and waited, because he had waited so long he found it easy to do. He must have had some sort of goofy grin on his face, because the trucker shook his head and mumbled something.

"That way," Tom said finally, pointing back to the east. "About five hundred miles up in the Brooks. I got abandoned at a cabin by my charter. I walked out."

"How long?"

"Took me a month, something like that. What's the date?"

"September 29. No, I mean, how long have you been back in those hills?"

"A little over a year. One winter."

"Sonofabitch." He shook his head. "Well, your walking days are over. Insurance says I can't pick up hitchhikers, but fuck that. This is a rescue. We're north of Coldfoot. You can call the troopers from there and sort this out."

The trucker helped him into his rig, put his pack in the back, in a sleeper cab. Zy jumped up and laid down on the floor. The trucker held out his hand, and Tom shook it, surprised not at the hard muscles of the man, but at the warmth of his skin, of the human contact. Tom got in.

"My name's Greg," the trucker said. "I work out

of Fairbanks, a run every week, sometimes two, been doing it on and off since the Pipeline got built."

"I appreciate the ride," Tom said.

The trucker eased the rig back onto the highway. Tom noticed that he shifted smoothly, not a jerky driver, in control. He had a rack of tapes and CDs on the console next to him, mostly books on tape, some movie sound tracks. Greg had a slight gut, muscled arms and solid shoulders, a few wrinkles around his eyes and a little gray in his beard. He had a black Caterpillar ball cap, until Tom realized the yellow lettering read "Dog," not "Cat."

"I'm Tom," he said, remembering the social custom: Guy introduces himself, you introduce yourself back. "Tom Foster. Got a house in Fairbanks myself."

"You got any family? Wife? Kids?"

"No kids," he said. "No wife. Some cousins back east, but I doubt they missed me."

"No one went looking for you? Nobody at work?"

Tom shrugged. "I'm a day trader, stock markets. I got a little ahead in the market and figured I'd take a break." He shook his head. "Took more of one than I realized. This . . . this old college friend has an old cabin, a miner's cabin and claim he inherited from family. An inholding in the park, claim and everything. He lets me go up there and work it so he can keep the claim up. He's back east, too." Tom felt the half-lies roll off his tongue like he almost believed them himself.

"Well, that bastard bush pilot shouldn't have forgotten you."

"Maybe something happened to him— a fire at his office, his plane crashed and he got killed. I'll sort it out, sue his ass if I have to."

"There you go."

Greg noticed Tom looking at the tapes again. "You want to listen to a book? I've got some Stephen King, Michael Connelly's latest—just started it but I could rewind to the first chapter."

Tom shook his head. "I'm kinda not used to words." He patted Zy's head. "My dog doesn't say much. Maybe some music?"

"Music works. I'm used to not talking too much myself," he said. "You need silence, you got it." Greg looked over at him. "A whole year in the wild, and you walked out." He shook his head. "Son of a bitch."

About an hour later, or maybe two, or maybe five— Tom had lost track of his sense of time—they pulled into Coldfoot. Greg said he could take a shower there ("My treat.") and he might have some clean clothes in his truck that Tom could borrow. While Greg went off to refuel, Tom took a shower.

Tom came out of the bathroom feeling lighter, as if the washing away of a year's dirt had relieved him of a few pounds. Greg's clean clothes felt stiff, alien, even though Tom could see Greg had given him his most tattered jeans, his most faded T-shirt and flannel shirt. Clean socks, clean underwear; he might as well have been reborn.

He found the trucker in the little café. He almost

gagged on the smell of cigarette smoke, the smell of other people. The conversation of the other truckers and diners hit him like storm surf, the conversation paused and everyone looked up at him, then back to their food and drinks and smokes.

Tom slid into the bench across the booth from Greg. The vinyl seat seemed bizarre under him; sitting across from another person seemed bizarre in itself. He set his hands at the table, looked across the table at Greg, around the room at the others, maybe a dozen people in all. A waitress came up to them, smiled at Tom. He almost gagged on her perfume, not the heaviness of it, for she didn't wear that much, or the pleasing scent, just the idea of it, a human and normal smell. She had that truckstop waitress look, the roadhouse glare that said she didn't take no shit, but underneath the fine wrinkles around her eyes and the graying red hair around her face, he realized that she was kind of pretty.

"I'm Mel, doll. You that guy that walked out of the wilderness?" she asked.

"Yeah. Name's Tom."

"Pretty amazing thing you did, Tom." She nodded, just slightly, in that old sourdough way that indicated, okay, you might have done something impressive. "You hungry, sweetheart?" She smiled, and it took him a few seconds to get the joke. "Dinner's on the house. You want a steak?"

A steak? Tom thought. He wanted a whole damn cow. He looked at the menu, at all the choices, and decided on steak, eggs, hash browns, cole slaw and a beer. Did they have beer? Of course they had beer. "And something for my dog out in the truck, maybe some scraps? He hasn't eaten in a while, too."

He tore through his meal, listening to Greg talk about driving the Haul Road, about some scary trips through whiteouts and avalanches, only after a while Tom didn't pay any attention. He'd lost the ebb and flow of conversation, of how humans interacted. When he finished his meal, his first beer, and had moved on to a second beer and the best damn cheesecake he'd ever had, the trooper came up to their table and sat down.

It took Tom a second to realize he was there, the guy had moved with such quiet grace, then another few seconds to realize he wasn't quite like the blur of other people in the room, bushrats and truckers and hunters. The trooper had on a bulky armored vest, a crisp blue shirt and dark tie, neatly pressed pants and a gear belt with almost as many gadgets as belt. Hartman, Tom read his nametag, Sgt. Hartman. Hartman pulled out a notebook and pen and laid them on the table.

"Heard you had a little adventure, sir."

"Tom. Tom Foster," he said. "Yeah, you could say that."

"Mind if I ask you a few questions? From what I hear, there might have been a crime involved."

"It's a crime to walk out of the wilderness?" Tom asked.

"No, that's an adventure, sir. It's a crime for someone to abandon you in the wilderness. Your bush pilot should have picked you up. We don't take that sort of thing lightly here, not in Alaska. You could have died."

"I know."

"I should follow up on that."

"I'd, uh, rather not go into the whole thing right now." Tom shook his head. "I'm a little confused, I think."

"I understand. Greg here says he can take you to Fairbanks, get you settled in, let you figure things out. Look, I know you've been through a lot, so I won't push it now, but the troopers would appreciate it if you'd talk to someone down in Fairbanks. Will you do that?"

"Sure, I guess. Yeah. Absolutely."

"Fine. I do need to see if there's an open search on you, though. You have some identification, something I could run through the computer, Mr. Foster?"

Tom nodded, handed him his beat-up old driver's license. The trooper looked at him with his beard and shaggy hair, at the photo of him clean shaven and with short hair, then nodded. Tom still had brown eyes, still had a mole on his forehead, a little scar under his right eye.

"I'll be right back," Hartman said. He came back a few minutes later, handed Tom back his license. "Well, your license is current, oddly enough. You'll be pleased to know that the state closed that search, though."

"They found me?" Tom asked.

"No. Presumptive death, sir. A jury declared you legally dead two months ago, cause of death exposure, probable location of death"—and he looked down at his notepad—"about three hundred miles west of here."

"I walked in from the east," Tom said quietly. "I don't know where the hell from, but I came in from the east."

"Well, you're not dead, either," Hartman said. He put on his hat. "Give us a call in Fairbanks and we'll get this straightened up. Welcome back to the living, sir. You've done a hell of a thing and you have my admiration. Hell of a thing."

The last leg between Coldfoot and Fairbanks went by swiftly. Tom chatted a bit with Greg, but mostly the long miles rolled on in silence. They pulled into Fairbanks late that night. Greg dropped Tom off on Airport Way, one of those tacky roads of strip malls, bars and cheap motels.

"Check in with the troopers," Greg told him, and to be polite, Tom agreed with him. He had no intention of visiting the troopers or the law, not just yet, although he figured sooner or later he'd have to. Tom believed in confronting his problems directly.

Tom walked down the street until he found a cash machine. Even though it seemed silly in the wilderness to have a wallet, all those miles he had carried it, that and a set of car keys, because he intended to return to civilization, and those things like credit cards and ATM cards would be useful. He slid his first ATM card into the slot, punched in his code, and heard the machine eat the card. ACCOUNT CLOSED, the screen read, CONTACT BANK FOR FURTHER INFORMA-

TION. Okay, he thought, he expected that: It had been his personal savings account set up at the same bank where he and Jackie had their main accounts. She would know about that one, would have closed it if he had died. *When* he died, he corrected himself.

Tom put in his second ATM card, his private one that Jackie didn't know about, statements sent to a P.O. box that Jackie didn't know about, either. WELCOME TOM FOSTER, the screen read after he punched in his PIN, and Tom smiled. It still held a few thousand dollars, little bonuses he had laundered out of his day trading. Tom withdrew three hundred dollars, enough walking-around money to do for half a week.

He found a motel down the block that would let him keep Zy in the room. The hotel took cash and didn't expect him to put down a credit card number. Tom let Zy in the room, got settled in, dropped his pack and then went out again. There was a Safeway down the street, open twenty-four hours. He picked up groceries, dog food for Zy, a new dog food bowl, soap and shampoo, a can of shaving foam, a twelve-pack of disposable razors and a cheap pair of barber scissors. The Safeway had a closeout sale on Alaska sweatshirts, sweatpants and T-shirts; he picked up a new outfit, new socks, new underwear, too.

Back in the motel room, Tom soaked in the bathtub until the water turned cold. He drained it, filled it up with hot water again and soaked more. He might have to take a dozen such baths before a year of dirt washed away, but at least he felt human, felt clean.

Tom opened up the door to the bathroom to let

the steam out, put on his new sweatpants, new T-shirt, then went back into the bathroom. He looked at himself, at his thick beard and scraggly hair.

He snipped away as much of his beard with the scissors as he could, getting the hair down as close as he could cut. Tom washed his face and soaked the beard with shaving foam and began scraping with the razors. It took three razors to get the beard totally shaved, his face completely bare. Tom hadn't really looked at himself out there in the wild, had never thought of what he looked like or how he appeared. Looking at himself clean shaven again, he recognized himself, knew himself. Tom smiled. It was important to know who he was. It would be important for others to recognize him, too.

The next morning he rose with the sun. Long ago he had given up clocks, had fallen into a schedule where he went to bed with the sun and rose with the sun. For the past year his schedule had been the same: get up, walk around with Zy, check his traps, check the area, keep walking. He and the dog needed a walk, long walks, actually; he no longer could start the day without one. They walked up and down the strip, two miles out, two miles back, checking out the area. He found one of those strip mall hair salons, one with a corny name like The Hair Force. It opened at ten, at least an hour to kill, so Tom and Zy walked two more miles, then Tom walked back to the motel, put the husky in the room and walked back to the salon. The stylist, a tall redhead with an extremely short pixie cut and twelve earrings, didn't even blink at the shagginess of his coiffure. Tom figured in a town one hop away from the bush, she probably saw a lot of heads looking as wild as his. On a whim he sprung for a manicure, too.

Just before noon, Tom checked out of the cheap motel. His bare face and close-cropped hair felt strange still, the new clothes strange, but it made him feel more civilized. It surprised him how quickly he had resettled into urban life: beard gone, hair cut, hands and feet scrubbed, another shower, and all his dirty and ratty clothes thrown out. Tom had even brushed Zy so the dog looked more domesticus and less lupus. Tom had on new underwear, new socks, new shirts and pants and a new hat. Thoreau had said to beware of enterprises requiring new clothes, and Tom smiled at that. Yeah, but sometimes you wore out your clothes. He had put a new edge on his sheath knife, oiled his sheath, cleaned the knife. He still kept his old pack and his worn boots, because they had a lot of wear left in them, and once you broke in a backpack and boots, it would be a shame to toss out all that work.

He had a wad of crisp new bills in his pocket, shiny dollar coins he hadn't seen a year ago and new quarters with new designs. The Cassull hung heavy in the top of his pack, easy to get at, not easily seen. He didn't know if it counted as a concealed weapon or not, and didn't give a damn either way. He'd cleaned and oiled the big revolver, too, bought a box of cartridges and put in three more rounds, with the hammer on an empty chamber. In his pocket he had six more.

Okay, he thought, now I'm ready to go home.

Walking west on Airport Way, Tom took a right on the road to the university, over the Chena River and then up Geist to Chena Ridge Road. As the road rose, he remembered running along the road over a year ago, in early fall, the aspen turning yellow, their leaves rattling in a slight breeze. He liked rising up out of the Fairbanks bowl, above the ice fog in the winter and to the homes and cabins with the better view, the better air. Up and up again.

He got that feeling you'd sometimes get when you returned someplace long familiar after being away a time, like everyone and everything had forgotten you and you felt like an alien. Well, they had forgotten him, and if that trooper was right, took him for dead. Tom didn't see how Jackie could do that to him, how she could just give up. Maybe she'd died, too, or something had happened. Heading home, now within a mile of his old house, he thought about how he'd play it, how he would know the truth when he knocked on the door. It all depended on who would be home, midafternoon on a nice Saturday, on who would answer the door.

As he came around that last bend up to his house, where he could see the long driveway going up to his house, in the little parking pad halfway up he saw the Benz SUV, his car, the one he'd bought when he made his first $100,000 from day trading—his first clear one-hundred-grand profit. The SUV had been parked nose out, like he always parked it, so in a snowstorm it didn't take much to get the all-wheel-drive rig punching through drifts. Tom felt the key chain in his pocket, the big Mercedes key on the end of it and the car alarm beeper. He'd bought a new battery for that, too. A couple of times walking out of the wilderness he'd thought of chucking that key chain, but like his credit cards, it had been a talisman of civilization to keep him going.

"Stay," he said to Zy, and the big husky sat down next to the Benz. No sense risking the dog up there at the house, Tom thought.

He came up on the far side of the drive, in the blind spot you couldn't see from the front door and the front window. For a while that had bugged him, that an intruder could be almost right up to the house before being spotted, until he'd gotten Zy, and realized that anyone crunching up the gravel driveway, or making snow creak in the winter, would alert the dog. Would she have gotten a new dog? Probably not. She was a cat type, and cats didn't bark.

Up at the top of the drive, nose in, someone had parked a new vehicle. A cherry-red Hummer, for Christ's sake, he saw, a damned good military truck but overpriced for what you got. The Hummer didn't look like it had gone through a Fairbanks winter or breakup yet: no windshield pings, no gravel-pocked side panels.

Tom kept to the side of the drive, up to the door and the big elderberry bush there. He set down his pack, took out the Cassull, put the pack back on and loaded the last round in the handgun. A round before the hammer, totally unsafe, and ready to fire. Tom knocked on the door with the butt of the grip and then clicked off the safety.

He had played this out, too, thought about what he'd do if the door opened to whom he hoped wouldn't be there. Shoot quickly, he had decided, blow the fucker away. Don't think, don't process more information than necessary, just squeeze the trigger and go. So when the door opened he surprised himself when he thought a moment more.

"Hang on, honey," the man said, opening the door, his back to Tom and looking at someone inside before the man turned and said to Tom, "Hey, what do you want?" Only, he didn't quite say "want," just a sort of "wh—" sound, like he'd all of a sudden swallowed his own balls.

"Frank," Tom said. "How's it going?"

Later, Tom would tell himself he hesitated because he wanted Frank to know before he died. He wanted Frank to understand that his plan had failed, that flying his best friend over five hundred miles into the wilderness and abandoning him had been a coward's way of killing someone, and that it hadn't worked. He wanted Frank to know just a bit of the terror Tom had felt the last year and a half, never knowing if he would survive. He had. He wanted Frank to know that, too.

Jackie came out into the foyer then, out from the house, his house, behind Frank. She'd cut her hair, and that said something to Tom, too, because Jackie had always liked her hair long and Tom didn't care how she wore it, as long as she wore it how she wanted. Only Frank liked short hair on women, really short, and she'd cropped it for him. She came up from behind Frank, dressed in the little short kimono Tom had given her on their fifth anniversary. She'd never worn it for him, Tom thought, because it was too short, too sexy.

"Frank, pay the newspaper carrier and—" Jackie got that gonads-in-the-mouth look, too. "Oh my. Tom."

"Hey, Jackie." Tom smiled and raised up the Cassull, a bead on Frank's chest, but with those .454 rounds, one shot through his lungs ought to keep going and blow Jackie away, too. He had a nice clean shot.

"I . . . Frank said you'd vanished, that he'd looked all over the Brooks and found your camp and Zy but not your body."

Tom shook his head slightly, to let her know he didn't believe her bullshit, and kept the gun steady. He thought he had better shoot before he thought too much longer and confused himself. When he bagged that first moose, the big fat fall one, he had done so only after missing three moose and using up twelve rounds of precious ammunition. He made the shot because he didn't think, just felt. And damn it, here he was thinking.

He liked the look on their faces, liked the way piss rolled down Jackie's nice tan legs, legs tanned from hours in the fake-and-bake bed. He liked how the piss steamed in the cool air coming through the open door. Tom pulled back on the hammer; in all that thinking, he couldn't remember if he had put a round back in the empty chamber or not.

The sound of that hammer cocking back was a lot more subtle than jacking a round into a pump shotgun, but just as effective. Frank's lips quivered a bit and his hands shook and his legs shook.

"Now Tom," Frank said. "Uh, Tom, we can work somethin' out, c'mon—"

"Frank," Tom said, just the right intonation, like he had grown weary and didn't really want anymore of his bullshit.

Then Frank's bladder opened up, a nice satisfying stream easing down his sweatpants and damned if the asshole didn't let loose with his bowels, too. In that moment Tom understood it all, understood why he had walked out, why he had returned, why he had walked up the road to his house. He wanted to know. He wanted to understand who had left him for dead and how and why. In that tableau, his wife with his best friend, shitting his pants in the foyer of Tom's house, he understood.

Tom lowered the Cassull and uncocked the hammer. He put the safety back on and opened up the cylinder, emptying it. He put the cartridges in his pocket and handed the handgun butt first to Frank.

"Thanks for the loan of the Cassull, Frank," Tom said. "Saved my butt, it did. You could have left me a few more bullets, but what the hell. It turned out I came back with two extra." He jingled the key chain.

"Tom," Jackie said, "I—"

"Nice haircut, Jackie. Suits you fine. Suits me fine."

Tom turned away and walked down the driveway to the Benz. He clicked the remote and the doors unlocked. Zy stood up as he approached. Tom opened the back door, throwing out Jackie's crap on the ground, gym bag, racquetball racquet, and Zy jumped in. Tom got in, readjusted the seat and mirrors. In the rearview he could see Frank standing in the doorway, still looking at him, Frank holding that big Cassull. For a moment, Tom regretted giving it back, but hell, he'd done the honorable thing. He flipped through the CD collection, flung all Jackie's country western CDs out the window. Country. He hated the damn stuff, and thought Jackie did, too. He had thought a lot of things about Jackie that turned out to be wrong, it seemed.

"Up front," Tom said, patting the front seat, and Zy leaped over the console. Tom started the Benz, eased it into gear and drove down the driveway. He didn't have the slightest idea where he would go, and didn't care.

Tom had walked out of the wilderness and he could go anywhere he wanted.

Anywhere at all.

WAR CAN BE MURDER
Mike Doogan

Two men got out of the Jeep and walked toward the building. Their fleece-lined leather boots squeaked on the snow. One of the men was young, stocky and black. The other was old, thin and white. Both men wore olive drab wool pants, duffel coats and knit wool caps. The black man rolled forward onto his toes with each step, like he was about to leap into space. The white man's gait was something between a saunter and a stagger. Their breath escaped in white puffs. Their heads were burrowed down into their collars and their hands were jammed into the pockets of their coats.

"Kee-rist, it's cold," the black man said.

Their Jeep ticked loudly as it cooled. The building they approached was part log cabin and part Quonset hut with a shacky plywood porch tacked onto the front. Yellow light leaked from three small windows. Smoke plumed from a metal pipe punched through its tin roof. A sign beside the door showed a black cat sitting on a white crescent, the words CAROLINA MOON lettered beneath.

"You sure we want to go in here?" the black man asked.

"Have to," the white man said. "I've got an investment to protect."

They hurried through the door and shut it quickly behind them. They were standing in a fair-sized room that held a half-dozen tables and a big bar. They were the only ones in the room. The room smelled of cigarette smoke, stale beer and desperation. The white man led the way past the bar and through a door, turned left and walked down a dark hallway toward the light spilling from another open door.

The light came from a small room that held a big bed and four people not looking at the corpse on the floor. One, a big, red-haired guy, was dressed in olive drab with a black band around one biceps that read "MP" in white letters. The other man was short, plump and fair-haired, dressed in brown. Both wore guns on their hips. One of the women was small and temporarily blond, wearing a red robe that didn't hide much. The other woman was tall, black and regal as Cleopatra meeting Caesar.

"I tole you, he give me a couple of bucks and said I should go get some supper at Leroy's," the temporary blond was saying.

" 'Lo, Zulu," the thin man said, nodding to the black woman.

"Mister Sam," she replied.

"What the hell are you doing here, soldier?" the MP barked.

"That's *Sergeant*," the thin man said cheerfully. He nodded to the plump man. "Marshal Olson," he said. "Damn cold night to be dragged out into, isn't it?"

"So it is, Sergeant Hammett," the plump man said. "So it is." He shrugged toward the corpse on the floor. "Even colder where he is, you betcha."

"Look you," the MP said, "I'm ordering you to leave. And take that dinge with you. This here's a military investigation, and if you upstuck it, I'll throw you in the stockade."

"If I what it?" Hammett asked.

"Upstuck," the MP grated.

"Upstuck?" Hammett asked. "Anybody got any idea what he's talking about?"

"I think he means 'obstruct'," the black man said.

"Why thank you, Clarence," Hammett said. He pointed to the black man. "My companion is Clarence Jefferson Delight. You might know him better as Little Sugar Delight. Fought Tony Zale to a draw just before the war. Had twenty-seven—that's right, isn't it Clarence?—twenty-seven professional fights without a loss. Not bad for a dinge, eh?" To the plump man, he said, "It's been a while since I was involved in this sort of thing, Oscar, but I believe that as the U.S. Marshal you're the one with jurisdiction here." To the MP, he said, "Which means you can take your order and stick it where the sun don't shine."

The MP started forward. Hammett waited for him with arms hanging loosely at his sides. The marshal stepped forward and put a hand on the MP's chest.

"Maybe you'd better go cool off, fella," he said. "Maybe go radio headquarters for instructions while I talk to these folks here."

The MP hesitated, relaxed, said, "Right you are, Marshal," and left the room.

"Maybe we should all go into the other room," the marshal said. The others began to file out. Hammett crouched next to the corpse, which lay on its back, arms outflung, completely naked. He was a young, slim, sandy-haired fellow with blue eyes and full lips. His head lay over on his shoulder, the neck bent much farther than it should have been. Hammett laid a hand on the corpse's chest.

"Give me a hand, Oscar, and we'll roll him over," he said.

The two men rolled the corpse onto its stomach. Hammett looked it up and down, grunted, and they rolled it back over.

"You might want to make sure a doctor examines that corpse," he said as the two men walked toward the barroom. "I think you'll find he was here to receive rather than give."

The temporary blond told a simple story. A soldier had come into her room, given her $2 and told her to get something to eat.

"He said don't come back for an hour," she said.

She'd gone out the back door, she said, shooting a nervous look at the black woman, so she wouldn't have to answer any questions. When she returned she'd found the soldier naked and dead.

"She told me," the black woman said to the marshal, "and I sent someone for you."

"What did you have to eat?" Hammett asked the temporary blond.

"Leroy said it was beefsteak, but I think it was part of one of them moose," she said. "And some mushy canned peas and a piece of chocolate cake. I think it give me the heartburn. That or the body."

"That's a story that should be easy enough to check out," Hammett said.

"And what about you, Zulu?" the marshal asked.

"I was in the office or behind the bar all night, Mister Olson," the black woman said. "That gentleman came in, had a drink, paid the usual fee and asked for a girl. When I asked him which one, he said it didn't matter. So I sent him back to Daphne."

"Seen him before?" the marshal asked.

"Lots of men come through here," Zulu said. "But I think he'd been here before."

"He done the same thing with me maybe three, four times before," the temporary blond said. "With some a the other girls, too." She shot another nervous look at the black woman. "We talk sometimes, ya know."

"Notice anybody in particular in here tonight?" the marshal said.

"Quite a few people in here tonight," Zulu said. "Some for the music, some for other things. Maybe thirty people in here when the body was found. I think maybe one of them is on the city council. And there was that banker . . ."

"That's enough of that," the marshal said.

"And he could have let anybody in through the back door," Zulu said.

The red-haired MP came back into the barroom, chased by a blast of cold air.

"The major wants me to bring the whore in to the base," he said to the marshal.

"I don't think Daphne wants to go anywhere with you, young man," Zulu said.

"I don't care what a whore thinks," the MP said.

Zulu leaned across the bar and very deliberately slapped the MP across the face. He lunged for her. Hammett stuck a shoulder into his chest and the marshal grabbed his arm.

"You probably don't remember me, Tobin," Hammett said, leaning into the MP, "but I remember when you were just a kid on the black-and-blue squad in San Francisco. I heard you did something that got you thrown out of the cops just before the war. I don't remember what. What was it you did to get tossed off the force?"

"Fuck you," the MP said. "How do you know so much, anyway?"

"I was with the Pinks for a while," Hammett said. "I know some people."

"You can relax now, son," the marshal said to the MP. "Nobody roughs up Zulu when I'm around. You go tell your major that if he wants to be involved in this investigation he should speak to me directly. Now beat it."

"I'm too old for this nonsense," Hammett said after the MP left, "but you can't have people beating up your partner. It's bad for business."

"There ain't going to be any business for a while," the marshal said. "Until we get to the bottom of this, you're closed, Zulu. I'll roust somebody out and have 'em collect the body. Otherwise, keep people out of that room until I tell you different."

With that, he left.

"I believe I'll have a drink now, Zulu," Hammett said.

"You heard the marshal," the black woman said."We're closed."

"But I'm your partner," Hammett said, grinning.

"Silent partner," she said. "I guess you forgot the silent part."

"Now there's gratitude for you, Clarence," Hammett said. "She begs me for money to open this place and now that she has my money she doesn't want anything to do with me. Think what I'm risking. Why, if my friends in Hollywood knew I was part owner of a cathouse . . ."

"They'd all be lining up three-deep for free booze and free nooky," Zulu said. "Now you two skedaddle. I've got to get Daphne moved to another room, and I'll have big, clumsy white folk tracking in and out of here all night. I'll be speaking to you later, Mister Sam."

The two men went back out into the cold.

"Little Sugar Delight?" the black man said. "Tony Zale? Why do you want to be telling such stories?"

"Why, Clarence," Hammett said, "think how boring life would be if we didn't all make up stories."

The black man slid behind the wheel and punched the starter. The engine whirred and whined and exploded into life.

"You can drop me back at the Lido Gardens,"

Hammett said. "I have a weekend pass and I believe there's a nurse who's just about drunk enough by now."

Hammett awoke the next morning alone, sprawled fully clothed on the bed of a small, spare hotel room. One boot lay on its side on the floor. The other was still on his left foot. He raised himself slowly to a sitting position. The steam radiator hissed and somewhere outside the frosted-over window a horn honked. Hammett groaned loudly as he bent down to remove his boot. He pulled off both socks, then took two steps across the bare, cold floor to a small table, poured himself a glass of water from a pitcher and drank it. Then another. He took the empty glass over to where his coat dangled from the back of a chair and rummaged around in the pockets until he came up with a small bottle of whiskey. He poured some into the glass, drank it and shuddered.

"The beginning of another perfect day," he said aloud.

He walked to the washstand and peered into the mirror. The face that looked back was pale and narrow, topped by crew-cut gray hair. He had baggy, hound-dog brown eyes and a full, salt-and-pepper mustache trimmed at the corners of a wide mouth. He took off his shirt and regarded his pipe-stem arms and sunken chest.

"Look out, Tojo," he said.

He walked to the other side of the bed, opened a small leather valise and took out a musette bag. Back at the washstand, he reached into his mouth and removed a full set of false teeth. His cheeks, already sunken, collapsed completely. He brushed the false teeth vigorously and replaced them in his mouth. He shaved. Then he took clean underwear from the valise, left the room and walked down the hall toward the bathroom. About halfway down the hall, a small, dark-haired man lay snoring on the floor. He smelled of alcohol and vomit. Hammett stepped over him and continued to the bathroom.

After bathing, Hammett returned to his room, put on a clean shirt and walked down a flight of stairs to the lobby. He went through a door marked CAFÉ and sat at the counter. A clock next to the cash register read 11:45. A hard-faced woman put a thick cup down in front of him and filled it with coffee. Hammett took a pair of eyeglasses out of his shirt pocket and consulted the gravy-stained menu.

"Breakfast or lunch?" he asked the hard-faced woman.

"Suit yourself," she said.

"I'll have the sourdough pancakes, a couple of eggs over easy and orange juice," Hammett said. "Coffee, too."

"Hey, are these real eggs?" asked a well-dressed, middle-aged man sitting a few stools down. The left arm of his suit coat was empty and pinned to his lapel.

The hard-faced women blew air through her lips.

"Cheechakos," she said. "A course they're real eggs. Real butter, too. This here's a war zone, you know."

She yelled Hammett's order through a serving hatch to the Indian cook.

"Can't get this food back home?" Hammett asked the one-armed man.

"Ration cards," the man replied. "Or the black market."

"Much money in the black market?" Hammett asked.

The one-armed man made a sour face.

"Guess so," he said. "You can get most anything off the back of a truck, most of it with military markings. And they say the high society parties are all catered by Uncle Sam. But I wouldn't know for certain." He flicked his empty sleeve. "Got this at Midway. I'm not buying at no goddamn black market."

A boy selling newspapers came in off the street. Hammett gave him a dime and took a newspaper, which was cold to the touch.

"Budapest Surrenders!" the headline proclaimed.

A small article said the previous night's temperature had reached twenty-eight below zero, the coldest of the winter. In the lower, right-hand corner of the front page was a table headed "Road to Berlin," It showed that allied troops were 32 miles away at Zellin on the eastern front, 304 miles away at Kleve on the western front and 504 miles away at the Reno River on the Italian Front.

The hard-faced woman put a plate of pancakes and eggs in front of Hammett. As he ate them he read that the Ice Carnival had donated $1,100 in proceeds to the Infantile Paralysis Fund, the Pribilof Five—

two guitars, a banjo, an accordion and a fiddle—had played at the USO log cabin and Jimmy Foxx had re-signed with the Phillies. He finished his meal, put a 50-cent piece next to his plate, and stood up.

"Where do you think you are, mister?" the hard-faced woman said. "Seattle? That'll be one dollar."

"Whew!" the one-armed man said.

Hammett dug out a dollar, handed it to the woman and left the 50-cent piece on the counter.

"Wait'll you have a drink," he said to the one-armed man.

Hammett walked across the lobby to the hotel desk and asked the clerk for the telephone. He consulted the slim telephone book, dialed, identified himself and waited.

"Oscar," he said. "Sam Hammett. Has the doctor looked at that corpse from last night? Uh-huh. Uh-huh. Was I right about him? I see. You found out his name yet and where he was assigned? A sergeant? That kid was a sergeant? What's this man's army coming to? And he was in supply? Nope, I don't know anybody over there. But if you want, I can have a word with General Johnson. Okay. How about the Carolina Moon? Can Zulu open up again? Come on, Oscar. Be reasonable. They didn't have anything to do with the killing. All right then. I guess we'd better hope you find the killer soon. See you. Oscar. 'Bye."

Hammett returned to his room, put on his overcoat and went out of the hotel. The air was warmer than it had been the night before, but not warm. He walked several blocks along the street, moving slowly over the hard-packed snow. He passed mostly one- or two-story wooden buildings, many of them hotels, bars or cafés. He counted seven buildings under construction. A few automobiles of prewar vintage passed him, along with several Jeeps and a new, olive drab staff car. He passed many people on foot, most of them men in work clothes or uniforms. When his cheeks began to get numb, he turned left, then left again and walked back toward the hotel. A couple of blocks short of his destination, he turned left again, crossed the street and went into a small shop with BOOK CACHE painted on its window. He browsed among the tables of books, picked one up and walked to the counter.

"Whatya got there?" the woman behind the counter asked. Her hair as nearly as gray as Hammett's. "*Theoretical Principles of Marxism* by V. I. Lenin." She smiled. "That sounds like a thriller. Buy or rent?"

"Rent," Hammett said.

"Probably won't get much call for this," the woman said. "How about ten cents for a week?"

"Better make it two weeks," Hammett said, handing her a quarter. "This isn't easy reading."

The woman wrote the book's title, Hammett's name and barracks number and the rental period down in a register, gave him a nickel back, and smiled again.

"Aren't you a little old to be a soldier?" she asked.

"I was twenty-one when I enlisted," he said, grinning. "War ages a man."

When it came time to turn for his hotel, Hammett

walked on. Two blocks later he was at a small wooden building with a sign over the door that read MILITARY POLICE.

"I'm looking for the duty officer," he told the MP on the desk. A young lieutenant came out of an office in the back.

"Sam Hammett of General Johnson's staff," Hammett said. "I'm working on a piece for *Army Up North* about military policing and I need some information."

"Don't you salute officers on General Johnson's staff?" the lieutenant snapped.

"Not when we're off duty and out of uniform, sir," Hammett said. "As I'm certain they taught you in OCS, sir."

The two men looked at one another for a minute, then the lieutenant blinked and said, "What can I do for you, Sergeant?"

"I need some information on staffing levels, sir," Hammett said. "For instance, how many men did you have on duty here in Anchorage last night, sir?"

Each successive "sir" seemed to make the lieutenant more at ease.

"I'm not sure," he said. "But if you'd like to step back into the office, we can look at the duty roster."

Hammett looked at the roster. Tobin's name wasn't on it. He took a notebook out of his coat pocket and wrote in it.

"Thank you, sir," he said. "Now I'll need your name and hometown. For the article."

Back at the hotel, Hammett removed his coat and boots. He poured some whiskey into the glass, filled it with water, lay down on the bed and began writing a letter.

"Dear Lillian," it began. "I am back in Anchorage and have probably seen the end of my posting to the Aleutians."

When he'd finished the letter, he made himself another drink and picked up his book. Within five minutes he was snoring.

He dreamed he was working for the Pinkerton National Detective Agency again, paired with a big Irish kid named Michael Carey on the Fatty Arbuckle case. He dreamed he was at the Stork Club, arguing with Hemingway about the Spanish Civil War. He dreamed he was in a watering hole on Lombard with an older Carey, who pointed out red-haired Billy Tobin and said something Hammett couldn't make out. He dreamed he was locked in his room on Post Street, drinking and writing *The Big Knockover*. His wife, Josie, was pounding on the door, asking for more money for herself and his daughters.

"Hey mister, wake up." It was the desk clerk's voice. He pounded on the door again. "Wake up, mister."

"What do you want?" Hammett called.

"You got a visitor downstairs. A shine."

Hammett got up from the bed and pulled the door open.

"Go get my visitor and bring him up," he said.

The desk clerk returned with the black man right behind him.

"Clarence, this is the desk clerk," Hammett said. "What's your name?"

"Joe," the desk clerk said.

"Joe," Hammett said, "this is Clarence 'Big Stick' LeBeau. Until the war came along he played third base for the Birmingham Black Barons of the Negro league. Hit thirty home runs or more in seven—it was seven, wasn't it, Clarence?—straight seasons. If it weren't for the color line, he'd have been playing for the Yankees. Not bad for a shine, huh?"

"I didn't mean nothing by that, mister," the desk clerk said. "You neither, Clarence." His eyes darted this way and that. "I got to get back to the desk," he said, and scurried off.

"Welcome to my castle," Hammett said, stepping aside to let the black man in. "What brings you here?"

"I've got to get started to Florida for spring training," the black man said. "The things you come up with. I didn't know white folk knew anything about the Birmingham Black Barons. And why do you keep calling me Clarence?"

"It suits you better than Don Miller," Hammett said. "And it keeps everybody guessing. Confusion to the enemy."

"You been drinking?" Miller said.

"A little," Hammett said. "You want a nip?" Miller shook his head. "But I've been sleeping more. The old need their sleep. What brings you here?"

"I was at the magazine office working on the illustrations for that frostbite article when I was called into the presence of Major General Davenport Johnson himself. He said you'd promised to go to a party tonight at some banker's house, and since he knew what an irresponsible s.o.b. you were—those were his words—he was ordering me to make sure you got there. Party starts in half an hour, so you'd better get cleaned up."

"I'm not going to any goddamn party at any goddamn banker's house," Hammett said. "I'm going to the Lido Gardens and the South Seas and maybe the Owl Club."

"This is Little Sugar Delight you're talking to, remember," Miller said. "You're going to the party if I have to carry you. General's orders."

"General's orders," Hammett said, and laughed. "That'll teach me to be famous." He took off his shirt, washed his face and hands, put the shirt back on, knotted a tie around his neck, put on his uniform jacket and a pair of glistening black shoes that he took from the valise and picked up his overcoat.

"All right, Little Sugar," he said, "let's go entertain the cream of Anchorage society."

Hammett got out of the Jeep in front of a two-story wooden house. Light spilled from all the windows and the cold air carried the muffled murmur of voices.

"You can go on about your business," he told Miller. "I'll walk back to town."

"It must be twenty below, Sam," Miller said.

"Nearer thirty, I expect," Hammett said. "But it's only a half-dozen blocks and I like to walk."

Indoors, the temperature was 110 degrees warmer. Men in suits and uniforms stood around drinking, talking and sweating. Among them was a sprinkling of overdressed women with carefully done-up hair. A horse-faced woman wearing what might have been real diamonds and showing a lot of cleavage walked up to Hammett.

"Aren't you Dashiell Hammett, the writer?" she asked.

Hammett stared down the front of her dress.

"Actually, I'm Samuel Hammett, the drunkard," he said after several seconds. "Where might I find a drink?"

Hammett quickly downed a drink and picked up another. The woman led him to where a large group, all wearing civilian clothes, was talking about the war.

"I tell you," a big, bluff man with dark, wavy hair was saying, "we are winning this war because we believe in freedom and democracy."

Everyone nodded.

"And free enterprise, whatever Roosevelt might think," said another man.

Everyone nodded again.

"What do you think, Dashiell?" the woman asked.

Hammett finished his drink. His eyes were bright and he had a little smile on his lips.

"I think I need another drink," he said.

"No," the woman said, "about the war."

"Oh, that," Hammett said. "First of all, we're not winning the war. Not by ourselves. We've got a lot of help. The Soviets, for example, have done much of the dying for us. Second, the part of the war we are winning we're winning because we can make more tanks and airplanes and bombs than the Germans and the Japs can. We're not winning because our ideas are better than theirs. We're winning because we're drowning the sonsabitches in metal."

When he stopped talking, the entire room was quiet.

"That was quite a speech," the woman said, her voice much less friendly than it had been.

"You'd have been better off just giving me another drink," Hammett said. "But don't worry. I can get it myself."

He was looking at a painting of a moose when a slim, curly-haired fellow who couldn't have been more than thirty walked up to him. He had a major's oak leaves on his shoulders.

"That was quite a speech, soldier," the major said. "What's an NCO doing at this party, anyway?"

"Ask the general," Hammett said.

"Oh, that's right, you're Hammett, the hero of the morale tour." The major took a drink from the glass he was holding. "You must be something on a morale tour with speeches like that." When Hammett said nothing, the major went on, "I hear you're involved in the murder of one of my sergeants."

Hammett laughed. "I don't know about involved," he said, "but I've got a fair idea who did it."

The major moved closer to Hammett.

"I think you'll find that in the army, it's safer to mind your own business," he said. "Much safer."

Hammett thrust his face into the major's face and opened his mouth to speak, but was interrupted by another voice.

"Ah, Sergeant Hammett," the voice said, "I see

you've met Major Allen. The major's the head of supply out at the fort."

"Thanks for clearing that up, General," Hammett
said. "I thought maybe he was somebody's kid and
these were his pajamas."

The major's face reddened and his mouth opened.

"Sergeant!" the general barked. "Do you know the
punishment for insubordination?"

"Sorry, General, Major," Hammett said. "This
whiskey just plays hob with my ordinarily high re-
gard for military discipline."

The major stomped off.

"That mouth of yours will get you into trouble one
day, Sergeant," the general said. He sounded as if he
were trying hard not to laugh.

"Yes, sir," Hammett said. "But he is a jumped-up
little turd."

"Yes, he is that," the general said. "Regular army.
His father was regular army, too. Chief of supply at
the Presidio. Did very well for himself. Retired to a
very nice home on Nob Hill. This one's following in
the family footsteps. All polish and connections.
There, see? See how politely he takes his leave of
the hostess. Now you behave yourself." The general
looked at the picture of the moose. "Damned odd
animal, isn't it?" he said, and moved off.

The general left the party a half hour later and
Hammett a few minutes after that. He made his way
down the short, icy walkway and, as he turned left,
his feet flew out from under him. As he fell he heard
three loud explosions. Something whirred past his
ear. He twisted so that he landed on his side and

rolled behind a car parked at the curb. He heard people boil out of the house behind him.

"What was that?" they called. And, "Are you all right?"

Hammett got slowly to his feet. There were no more shots.

"I'm fine," he called. "But I could use a lift downtown, if anyone is headed that way."

It was nearly midnight when Hammett walked into the smoke and noise of the Lido Gardens. A four-piece band was making a racket in one corner, and a table full of WACs was getting a big play from about twice as many men in the other. Hammett navigated his way across the room to the bar and ordered a whiskey.

"Not bad for a drunk," he said to himself and turned to survey the room. His elbow hit the shoulder of the man next to him. The man spilled some of his beer on the bar.

"Hey, watch it, you old bastard," the man growled, looking up. A broad smile split his face. "Well if it isn't Dash Hammett, the worst man on a stakeout I ever saw. What are you doing here at the end of the earth?"

"Dispensing propaganda and nursemaiding Hollywood stars," Hammett said. "Isn't that why every man goes to war? And what about you, Carey? The Pinks finally figure out how worthless you are and let you go?"

The two men shook hands.

"No, it's a sad tale," the other man said. "A man

of my years should have been able to spend the war behind a desk, in civilian clothes. But then the army figured out that a lot of money was rolling around because of the war and that money might make people do some bad things." Both men laughed. "So they drafted me. Me, with my bad knees and failing eyesight. Said I had special qualifications. And here I am, back out in the field, chasing crooks. For even less money than the agency paid me."

"War is indeed hell," Hammett said. "Let me buy you a drink to ease the pain." He signaled to the bartender. When both men had fresh drinks, he asked, "What brings you to Alaska?"

"Well, you'll get a good laugh out of this," Carey said. "You'll never guess who we found as a supply sergeant at Fort Lewis. Bennie the Grab. And he had Spanish Pete Gomez and Fingers Malone as his corporals."

"Mother of god," Hammett said. "It's a surprise there was anything left worth stealing at that place."

"You know it, brother," Carey said. "So you can imagine how we felt when all of the paperwork checked out. Bennie and the boys wouldn't have gotten much more than a year in the brig for false swearing when they joined up if it hadn't been for some smart young pencil pusher. He figured out they were sending a lot of food and not much of anything else to the 332nd here at Fort Richardson."

"Don't tell me," Hammett said. "There is no 332nd."

"That's right," Carey said. "The trucks were leaving the warehouses, but the goods for the 332nd weren't making it to the ships. There wasn't a restaurant or diner or private dinner party in the entire Pacific Northwest that didn't feature U.S. Army butter and beef. We scooped up Bennie and the others, a couple of captains, a major and a full-bird colonel. All the requisitions were signed by a Sergeant Prevo, and I drew the short straw and got sent up here to arrest him and roll things up at this end."

"It seems you got here just a bit late, Michael," Hammett said. "Because unless there are two supply sergeants named Prevo, your man got his neck broken in a gin mill last night. My gin mill, if it matters."

"This damned army," Carey said. "We didn't tell anybody at this end, because we didn't know who might be involved. And it looks like we'll never find out now, either."

"I don't know about that," Hammett said. "I need to know two things. Were the men running the supply operation at Fort Lewis regular army? And what was it a kid named Billy Tobin got kicked off the force in 'Frisco for? If you can answer those questions, I might be able to help you."

Before Hammett went down the hall to the bathroom the next morning, he took a small pistol from his valise and slipped it into the pocket of his pants. He left it there when he went downstairs for bacon and eggs. As he ate, he read an authoritative newspaper story about the Jap Army using babies as bayonet practice targets in Manila. He spent the rest of the day in his room, reading and dozing, leaving the room to take one telephone call. He ate no lunch. He looked

carefully up and down the hallway before his visit
to the bathroom. When his watch read 7:30, he got
fully dressed, packed his valise and sat on the bed.
Just at 9 P.M., there was a knock on his door.

"Mister," the desk clerk called. "You got a visitor.
The same fella."

Hammett walked downstairs and settled his bill
with the clerk. He and Miller went out and got into
a Jeep. Neither man said anything. The joints on the
far side of the city limits were doing big business as
they drove past. The Carolina Moon was the only
dark building. As they pulled up in front of it, Hammett said, "You might want to find yourself a quiet
spot to watch the proceedings."

"What you doing this for?" Miller asked. "Solving
murders isn't your business."

"This one is my business," Hammett said. "Zulu's
got to eat, and I want a return on my investment.
Nobody's making any money with the Moon closed."

"You and Miss Zulu more than just business part-
ners?" Miller asked.

"A gentleman wouldn't ask such a question,"
Hammett said, "and a gentleman certainly won't answer it."

Hammett hurried into the building. He had trouble
making out the people in the dimly lit barroom. Zulu
was there, and the temporary blond. The marshal.
The MP. Carey, a couple of tough-looking gents
Hammett didn't know and the major from the party.
The MP was standing at the bar, looking at himself
in a piece of mirror that hung behind it. Everyone
else was sitting. Hammett went around behind the bar,

took off his coat and laid it on the bar. He poured himself a drink and drank it off. The MP wandered over to stand next to the door to the hallway.

"I see you've got everyone assembled," Hammett said to Carey.

The investigator nodded.

"The major came to me," he said. "Said as it was his sergeant that was killed, he wanted to be in on this."

"That's one of the things that bothered me about this," Hammett said. "Major Allen seems to know things he shouldn't. For instance, Major, how did you know I was involved in this affair?"

The major was silent for a moment, then said, "I'm certain my friend Major Haynes of the military police must have mentioned your name to me."

"We'll leave that," Hammett said. "Because the other thing that bothered me came first. Oscar, did you call the MPs the night of the killing?"

The marshal shook his head.

"Then what was the sergeant doing here?"

"Said he was in the neighborhood," the marshal said.

"But Oscar," Hammett said, "don't the MPs always patrol in pairs on this side of the city limits?"

"They certainly do," the marshal said. "What about that, young fella?"

The MP looked at the marshal, then at Hammett.

"My partner got sick," he said. "I had to go it alone. Then I saw all them soldiers leaving here and came to see what was what."

"Michael?" Hammett said.

"Like you said, the duty roster said the sergeant wasn't even on duty that night," the investigator said.

Everyone was looking at the MP now. He didn't say anything.

"This is your case, Oscar," Hammett said, "so let me tell you a story.

"There's a ring of thieves operating out of Fort Lewis, pretending to send food to a phony outfit up here, then selling it on the black market. The ones doing the work were crooks from San Francisco. Tobin here would have known them from his time with the police there.

"Their man on this end, the fellow who was killed the other night, didn't seem to have any connection with them. Michael told me on the telephone today that he was from the Midwest and had never been arrested. He seemed to be just a harmless pansy who used the Moon to meet his boyfriend."

"That's disgusting," the major said.

"That's what happens when the army makes a place the dumping ground for all of its undesirables, Major," Hammett said. "What did you do to get sent here?"

"I volunteered," the major grated.

"I'll bet you did," Hammett said. "Anyway, last night Michael reminded me that Tobin here had been run off the San Francisco force for beating up a dancer at Finocchio's. He claimed the guy made a pass at him, but the inside story was that it was a lover's quarrel."

"That's a goddamn lie!" the MP shouted.

"It's just one coincidence too many," Hammett

said, his voice as hard as granite. "You know the San Francisco mob. They're stealing from the government. Prevo was in on the scheme. He was queer. You're queer. You're sewn up tight. What happened? He get cold feet and you had to kill him?"

The MP looked from one face to another in the room. Then he looked at Hammett.

"I didn't kill the guy," the MP said. "It was him." He pointed to the major.

Everyone looked at the major, then back at the MP. He was holding his automatic in his hand.

"That's not going to do you any good, young man," the marshal said. "This is Alaska. Where you going to run?"

The MP seemed not to hear him.

"I ain't no queer!" he shouted at Hammett. "I hate queers. I beat that guy up 'cause he made a pass at me, just like I said. I'd have killed him if I thought I'd get away with it. Here, I was just giving the major a little cover in case anything happened. Like the place got raided or something. Then the other day he told me some pal of his had warned him that they'd knocked over the Fort Lewis end of the deal and we were going to have to do something about his boyfriend. 'Jerry will talk,' he said. 'I know he will.' I told him I wasn't killing anybody. The stockade was better than the firing squad. So he comes out the back door of this place the other night and says he killed the pansy himself."

"That's a goddamn lie," the major shouted, leaping to his feet. "I don't even know this man. I've got a wife and baby at home. I'm no fairy."

"You're for it, Tobin," Hammett said to the MP. "He doesn't leave anything to chance. Why, he tried to shoot me last night just on the off chance I might know something. I'll bet he does have a wife and child. And I'll bet there's nothing to connect him to either you or the corpse. And there's the love letters Michael found in your footlocker."

"Love letters?" the MP said. "What love letters?" He looked at Hammett, then at the major. Understanding flooded his face.

"You set me up!" he screamed at the major. "You set me up as a fairy!"

The automatic barked. The slug seemed to pick the major up and hurl him backwards. The temporary blond screamed. All over the room, men were taking guns from holsters and pockets. They seemed to be moving in slow motion. The MP swung the gun toward Hammett.

"You should have kept your nose out of this," the MP said, leveling the automatic. His finger closed on the trigger.

Don Miller stepped out of the hallway behind the MP and laid a sap on the back of his head. The MP collapsed like he was filled with sawdust.

Miller and Hammett looked at one another for a long moment. Hammett took his hand off the pistol in the pocket of his coat.

"I think that calls for a drink," he said, pouring himself one.

The marshal was putting cuffs on the MP. Carey looked up from where the major lay and shook his head.

"I guess this means you'll be able to open up again, Zulu," Hammett said.

The following afternoon Miller found Hammett lying on a table in the cramped offices of the magazine *Army Up North*, reading Lenin.

"I've got some errands to run in town," he told Hammett.

"Fine by me," Hammett said, sitting up. "I've been thinking I'll put in my papers. The war can't last much longer and this looks like as close as I'll get to any action."

"You'd have been just as dead if that MP shot you as you would if it'd been a Jap bullet," Miller said.

"I suppose," Hammett said. "This morning the general told me that they were going to show Major Allen as killed in the line of duty. They'll give Tobin a quick trial and life in the stockade. The whole thing's being hushed up. The brass don't want to embarrass the major's father, and they don't want the scandal getting back to the President and Congress. This is the country I enlisted to protect?"

Miller shrugged. "I got to be going," he said.

"Right you are," Hammett said. "And by the way, thanks for stepping in last night. I didn't want to shoot that kid and I didn't want to get shot myself."

Miller turned to leave.

"I suppose I'll just give the Moon to Zulu if I go," Hammett said.

"That'd be real nice," Miller said over his shoulder.

He went out, got into a Jeep, drove downtown and parked. He walked into the federal building, climbed a set of stairs, walked down a hallway and went through an unmarked door without knocking. He sat in a chair and told the whole story to a man on the other side of the desk.

"That's all very interesting," the man said, "but did the subject say anything to you or anyone else about Marx, Lenin or communism?"

"Is that all you care about?" Miller asked. "I keep telling you, I've never heard him say anything about communism."

"You've got to understand," the man said. "This other matter just isn't important. The Director says we are already fighting the next war, the war against communism. This war is a triumph of truth, justice and the American way. And it's over."

Miller said nothing.

"You can let yourself out," the man said. Then he turned to his typewriter, rolled a form into it and began to type.

ALL THAT GLITTERS
Kate Grilley

"You're going *where*?"

"In *February*?"

"Kelly Ryan, are you demented? Even Alaskans don't stay in Alaska in February, they're all here in the Caribbean, on cruise ships."

"Wrong, Jerry," I said, glaring at Margo and Abby, who were falling all over themselves laughing at their own witless remarks, "real Alaskans have condos in Hawaii. Look, guys, all I asked was if anyone had a down coat I could borrow. I wasn't auditioning for Comedy Central." I set my iced tea glass on the round table. "It's a simple request. Does anyone have a down coat I can borrow?"

In St. Chris we pool our winter wear. I own a London Fog raincoat with a zip-in lining that's been borrowed so many times it could qualify for a platinum status in any frequent flyer program.

"Kel, I have a down coat," said Abby. "It's got a

fur-trimmed hood. Very *Doctor Zhivago*. I'll bring it tomorrow." She turned to Margo. "I know you have a scarf, hat and gloves. I borrowed them last year when I went to Dublin."

"All right, all right," said Margo. "Kel, I'll even take care of Minx while you're gone. On one condition. Dish, girl. Why are you going to Alaska in February? You're such a wimp, you complain if the temperature here dips down to sixty-eight."

"Last night it got so cold I turned on my electric blanket," said Jerry.

"Spare me, Jerry," said Margo, "last night's low was only seventy-one."

I signaled Carole, the Watering Hole waitress, to bring Jerry a drink and put it on my tab. "If you must know, I won second prize in the Christmas Jump-Up raffle. A one-week trip to Fur Rondy in Anchorage. It includes a dogsled ride with Libby Riddles, the first woman to win the Iditarod. I've always wanted to ride in a dogsled."

"I knew it," said Margo. "Only a cheapskate like you would leave St. Chris at the height of winter tourist season for a week in the frozen north. What was first prize?"

"Two weeks in Alaska," said Jerry with a grin.

I cancelled his drink order.

"Kel, bring me a pair of gold nugget studs from Alaska," said Margo.

"You'll be lucky to get a moose nugget key chain," I replied.

After a twenty-one hour trek—St. Chris to St. Thomas to Atlanta to Salt Lake and finally to Anchorage—I landed at Anchorage International Airport late Friday evening, Saturday dawn in St. Chris. My luggage was still circling Atlanta.

"We'll call you when it arrives," chirped the perky attendant at the airline counter. "Enjoy your stay in Alaska."

I gingerly skirted a stuffed polar bear standing on its hind legs, towering over me like an albino King Kong, then exited the airport into winter wonderland.

I tentatively drew a shallow breath, remembering February in Chicago when the sub-zero air felt like ice crystals stabbing my lungs. The dry Alaska air smelled like pine. I looked at boughs heavy with snow, tiny white lights glowing on every branch. It was a Christmas fantasy come to life. The pristine snow crunched under my feet as I headed toward a taxi.

From my room at the Hilton in downtown Anchorage, I overlooked the Fur Rondy midway, where parka-clad riders went 'round and 'round on the neon-lit Ferris wheel and played bumper cars under the stars. Next to the midway was a wooden grandstand where daily fur auctions would be held.

A flyer, handed to me when I checked in, listed the highpoints of the annual Alaskan winter carnival. Fur Rondy began in the 1930s to relieve cabin fever and celebrate the beginning of the end of winter. The first Rondy pin was designed in 1939, a lapel pin made out of leather and fur. I was laughingly warned by the woman at hotel reception that Keystone Kops were everywhere in downtown Anchorage, arresting

anyone found on the street without a Rondy pin. I
bought a collectible button depicting an Eskimo blanket toss and pinned it to the strap of my shoulder
bag.

Saturday night I joined three thousand people—
clutching tickets they'd queued to buy in early Janu-
ary—entering the ACS Warehouse, site of the fiftieth
anniversary Miners and Trappers Ball. Some said it
was the biggest costume ball outside of New Orleans.

The women eyed each other, trying to see what
was hidden beneath the scarves, parkas, down coats
and boots. One nudged another. "Vera wore that
dance hall costume last year. She won't win again."
After checking their outerwear, the men stroked their
beards—a beard, jeans and an old flannel shirt made
any man look and feel like a miner—and headed
straight for the bars. The women primped, adjusting
stockings, applying more rouge, fixing their hair before entering the party, bright smiles on their faces,
feet tapping to the music.

The warehouse was divided into four large rooms:
the main ballroom, the costume judging room, the
beard contest room and the coat check area at the
warehouse entrance. The crepe paper and balloon
decorations reminded me of a high school sock hop.
But no one was there to ooh and ahh over mere
window dressing, they were there to see and be seen,
consume drinks and snacks, have a five-dollar souve-
nir photo taken, enter the beard and costume con-
tests, then dance the night away.

It was like going back in time to the height of the
gold rush at one of Dawson City's famed dance halls.

I bought a beer and sat on the sidelines in the main ballroom, watching velvet-clad Victorian ladies and their top hatted gentlemen stroll leisurely from room to room, nodding to dance hall girls and miners. Signs on the walls lettered in a curlicued old-fashioned font warned one and all to BEWARE OF PICK-POCKETS AND LOOSE WOMEN. Men reading the signs surreptitiously patted their pockets.

Mingling with characters from the past were revelers in contemporary costumes: a trio decked in large silver tubes, looking like tin woodsmen from the *Wizard of Oz* but representing the Alaska Pipeline; a group in black pants and turtlenecks with wrist-length capes made of shimmering multihued foil strips were the famed northern lights. They moved about the ballroom with arms linked, dipping and swaying in a wave to the beat of a honky-tonk band.

I was heading for a fresh beer when an incessant *ding, ding, ding* growing louder behind me made me jump out of the way in the nick in time. A character dressed in spangled pink tights, ballet slippers, a long-sleeved leotard and gauzy tutu, sporting a long curly blond wig—looking like an angel hair–topped confection of virulent pink cotton candy—zipped past me on a foot-propelled scooter accessorized with cherry red–light flashing wheels. After pausing to fling a pink-gloved fistful of silver glitter in the air from a pouch strapped to the handlebars, it then moved on through the crowds. People stopped dancing to point, laugh and applaud.

I turned to a couple dressed as famed Dawson City dance hall girl Klondike Kate and her paramour, im-

presario Alexander Pantages. "What's the joke?" I
asked. "I don't get it."

They stopped laughing long enough to say, "It's
the parking fairy."

"The what?" I smiled. "I'm a tourist, tell me
more." While the man went off to register for the
Black Bear beard contest, the woman explained further as we waited in line for drinks. "The parking
fairy is an Anchorage institution. It began when
someone started putting money in downtown parking meters that were about to expire. Drove the cops
crazy because they couldn't write tickets. So they
threatened to arrest anyone caught plugging meters
on cars they didn't own. Alaskans are an independent lot. We just laughed at the cops and the parking
fairies kept on feeding the meters."

I thanked the woman by buying her a drink, and
watched the parking fairy zip from room to room,
sometimes crashing into partygoers who didn't jump
aside fast enough. With a sprinkle of glitter, a consol-
ing pat and a smiled apology, the parking fairy sped
on, wheel lights twinkling like rainbow-colored
fireflies.

"Around and around she goes and where she stops
nobody knows," muttered a middle-aged ginger-
bearded miner as he watched the parking fairy approach. He peered forlornly into the empty drink cup
clasped in his ink-stained fingers. The grimy hands
are a nice touch, I thought, he really looks like he's
been out in the gold fields working his claim. "I need
another drink, but I'm fresh outta tickets." The miner
reached in his jeans pocket and pulled out an elabo-

rately hand-tooled leather billfold, fattened by a thick wad of crisp bills. I was reminded of stories I'd read of gold rushers who blew the earnings of a summer of backbreaking labor on a winter of whiskey and women. The parking fairy showered us with glitter and sped on.

"Lady, I gotta take a whiz real bad. If you go get my drink tickets I'll buy you a drink, too," said the miner, waving a hundred-dollar bill in the air. "Hell, I'll buy all your friends a drink."

I held up my full beer bottle, declined his offer and quickly moved on.

The last call for drinks came at 1:30 A.M. In the dash to the bars for one for the road, the parking fairy swerved into a crush of partygoers, including the prizewinning northern lights group. They all fell to the ground in a tangle of arms, legs, velvet, foil and glitter. I saw Klondike Kate being helped to her feet by the ginger-bearded miner as I headed for the check room to reclaim Abby's down coat before the mass exit from the ball.

When I got back to my hotel, there was a message waiting from the airline. My luggage had finally arrived from Atlanta. I could pick it up between 7:30 and 9:00 Sunday morning when the airline counter was open for the morning outbound flight to Salt Lake City.

While the Miners and Trappers ballgoers were still tucked in bed with their aching heads, I went to the airport, arriving at 8 A.M. as the first frosty flakes of a predicted twelve-inch snow were beginning to fall.

I inched my way forward, the only one without

luggage, the last in a long line of outgoing passengers. "Can you believe we'll really be in Hawaii tonight? I've had enough of winter. Bring on those Mai Tai's," I overheard one woman exclaim. I finally arrived at the counter after waiting in line for forty-five minutes. Before I could request my luggage, I was interrupted by a slender, clean-shaven young man who had sprinted into the terminal, glistening snowflakes still intact on his jacket.

"Excuse me, lady, I gotta catch this plane," he said, tossing a backpack and large duffel onto the scale.

I stepped aside. I wasn't going anywhere. I'd been wearing the same jeans, turtleneck and St. Chris sweatshirt for three days; a few more minutes without my luggage wouldn't really matter.

"The flight to Salt Lake city is sold out, sir. We're boarding now."

"I've got a reservation," the young man told the airline clerk, and told her his name.

"Your final destination today, sir?"

"Honolulu," he replied.

"And how will you be paying for this, sir?"

"Cash."

He pulled a tooled leather billfold from his jacket pocket and began counting out crisp one-hundred-dollar bills.

"I'll be right back, sir," said the clerk, departing with the cash and a felt tip pen. "I have to get your change from the office. I'll need to see your photo ID before I can issue your boarding pass." She unlocked a door and slipped into an office behind the counter.

The young man pulled an ID from his pocket and stood with his back to me, drumming his fingertips on the counter. I noticed that some of the flakes hadn't yet melted on his jacket, yet sweat was trickling down my sides even though Abby's down coat was slung over my arm. I pulled the turtleneck away from my throat, took a deep breath, then fanned my face with my hand. It had been a long time since I'd lived with central heating.

A couple of minutes later the clerk returned to the counter, cash and pen in hand, as two men approached to stand on either side of the departing passenger.

"Keep your hands where we can see them, son."

Were these the Keystone Kops the hotel desk clerk had warned me about? I fingered the Rondy button pinned to my shoulder bag strap.

"What gives, man? I've got a plane to catch."

"Son, you're under arrest."

"What the hell for?" said the young man indignantly.

"Passing counterfeit currency." The men flashed their badges. "Secret Service. Possessing or passing phony money is a federal offense. You're looking at fifteen years in prison."

"But, but . . ." the young man kept saying as he was being read his rights. I knew the next words out of his mouth were going to be, "It's not my money." I also knew that when the ginger-bearded miner awoke, he wouldn't be filing a complaint with the police about his stolen billfold.

"You got something to say, son?"

I could see the wheels rapidly rotating inside the young man's head. He swallowed hard, then said, "I want to call a lawyer."

"Mind if we have a look inside your luggage?"

The young man reluctantly handed over his duffel bag key.

Inside the duffel, cushioned by a plastic trash bag filled with pink clothes and a blond wig, was a collapsible scooter, its bright red wheels flecked with silver glitter that looked like newly fallen snowflakes.

After the parking fairy was cuffed and taken away, I silently thanked my lucky stars that I'd declined the miner's drink offer, then stepped forward to claim my luggage.

LOSING STREAK
Sue Henry

Slack-jawed and oblivious to sidewalk pedestrians, Arnie Boyd slumped on a bench at the downtown Anchorage terminal, waiting for a noon People Mover that would carry him within walking distance of his shabby one-room efficiency in Muldoon. Reaching up with one large paw of a hand, he tugged at the brim of his cap. A small shower of cement dust fell from it, causing him to sneeze. Paroxysm over, he returned to his unmoving and dejected posture, trying to figure exactly why he had just lost his third job of the summer.

"Walking disaster," the foreman had called him between more colorful phrases, and ". . . clumsy bastard." As if he'd dropped the concrete block on purpose and it couldn't have happened to anyone. But he hadn't meant to cut a space too large for a window, or put a forklift through, rather than under, a pallet of five-gallon paint buckets, at his first two jobs either. Perhaps he *wasn't* cut out to work construction, as the boss had fervently assured him while nursing his injured foot, and voiced his opinion of Arnie's slim-to-none chance of future local hire. What the hell was he going to do now?

He had hoped the construction job would put enough in the bank for the winter, when jobs were hard to come by, to cover what unemployment wouldn't—a warm coat, and some boots that didn't leak. Easily entertained, he knew he would be content with a beer and a game of pool once or twice a week with the guys, if he could also somehow wrangle a secondhand television to while away the empty evenings. He sighed and shifted his weight on the bench, dreams of such luxury flittering away in view of his sudden, regrettable unemployed status. It just wasn't fair—not at all.

The bus rolled in. He rose and clumped up its steps in his battered work boots, paint and cement spattered, one leather lace knotted together in three places. Collapsing his lanky frame onto a seat, he dropped his lunch pail beside him and stared out the window, seeing little of the season's tourists and the lunchtime crowd of government workers spilling out of office buildings onto the sidewalks.

At the next stop several passengers climbed onto the bus, filling the few unoccupied seats. A heavy-set woman in sensible shoes paused in the aisle beside Arnie's seat and glared at his offending lunch pail.

"Excuse me."

Removing it to his knees, he clasped the pail be-

tween both hands, a reminder of what little it held—
last night's leftover spaghetti in a recycled plastic
margarine container and one small, slightly withered
apple. Knowing his larder was bare, he turned his
eyes back to the window and wondered if he should
eat the contents upon arrival, or save it for later.

The ride was long and the bus was soon traveling
through a residential area. As snug houses and neat
green lawns scrolled past, Arnie appraised them with
covetousness and not a little discouragement. He
imagined the interiors filled with comfortable furni-
ture—beds that didn't sag, chairs in which to relax,
televisions with VCRs, in front of which to enjoy the
movies he loved. It was hard enough to scrape together the price of his next meal and month-to-month
rent. Why, the price of a television alone would
pay for . . .

Detective Will Sinclair shook his head over the fin-
gerprint report on his desk, shrugged on his jacket,
and, with resignation, went out to pick up the perpe-
trator of the burglary he had investigated three days
earlier. From several minor scrapes with the law—
a bar fight, an arrest for disturbing the peace—he
remembered this perp, but never before for a
burglary.

He easily located Arnie Boyd in a ramshackle bar
in Muldoon, shooting pool, a Budweiser perched on
the edge of the table. The television and VCR that
had disappeared along with a collection of videotapes were found in Boyd's one-room apartment and
appropriated as evidence, eventually to be returned

to their owner. A couple of sacks' worth of groceries that had vanished from their owner's refrigerator and cupboard shelves were gone, except for a few cans of soup and beans. Forty-four dollars and eighty-two cents of a stolen $350 were retrieved from Boyd's pocket and a quarter from the rail of the pool table.

"Dumb," Sinclair told him, shaking his head and frowning as he fastened the handcuffs. "You knew your prints were in the system. Why the hell'd you leave 'em all over the place?"

A year later, Arnie found himself back in Muldoon, spending late afternoons sweeping up and restocking shelves for a convenience store and reporting to his parole officer once a week. He had tried for another construction job, but his negative references had preceded him everywhere, along with his arrest record. Minimum wage barely covered the rent on a damp room with a cot, a hot plate, and no windows in the basement of the store, but he got a break on wilted fruit and vegetables, stale bread, outdated cheese, and dented or label-less cans. The cot was more hammock than bed and the bare lightbulb that dangled from the ceiling was depressing, so he spent most of his spare time walking the streets, looking for odd jobs and shoving a finger in the coin return of any pay phone he passed.

Though he detested it, he usually did the store's restocking first thing in the afternoon. The sweeping came later, for when school let out the aisles filled up with kids on their way home, spending pocket

change on soda and sweets, tracking in dirt and lit-
tering sticky wrappers in the wake of their invasion.
Leaning on his broom, Arnie would cringe at the
noise and shoving, await their departure and try to
keep a protective eye on the store's enticing selection
of items full of enough sugar to give any self-
respecting dentist the shudders.

It was a gloomy Monday, with a whole week of
kids ahead, when a conversation caught his attention.

"Gimme a quarter, Danny?" whined a treble voice
from beyond the shelves.

"Haven't got one."

"You gotta lotta whole *dollars*."

"That's the magazine money I forgot to turn in."

"*Ple-e-eze!* I'll pay it back tomorrow, before you
gotta give it to Miss Daily."

"We-ell—okay."

Magazine money? Arnie sidled to the next aisle,
where he could see a scruffy kid in a blue sweatshirt
dig an envelope of bills from a jeans pocket and hand
a dollar to a smaller kid whose glasses covered half
his face.

"Promise?" Scruffy kept a tight hold on one end
of the bill until . . .

"Yeah, promise. Tomorrow morning."

Grabbing up their choice of candy, the two headed
for the cash register.

Magazines? They had to be selling subscriptions,
for he had seen the kid thrust several tens and ones
back into the envelope. And the teachers were col-
lecting the money? Hm-m-m! As Arnie swept the
floor and refilled the soda cooler he thought about

that, then, finished for the day, borrowed the crowbar he used for opening crates and a pair of canvas
gloves from a hook on the wall as he went out the
back door.

In the morning light that shone brightly on the remaining glass shards in the frame of a classroom
window of a Muldoon middle school, Detective Will
Sinclair examined several blue fibers, which hung
from one knife-point fragment. Denim, he decided,
retrieving them carefully to deposit in an evidence
bag. Two drawers of the teacher's locked desk had
been pried open with some force and $178 was
missing.

"Anything?" he asked the technician kneeling in
front of the drawer in a search for fingerprints.

"Just the teacher, from the look of these. Smudged.
Looks like whoever it was wore gloves." He whisked
more black powder on the drawer's edge with his
soft brush and frowned. "Yup, gloves. There's a
smear of blood, but no print in it."

Sinclair turned his attention to small spatters of
blood on the tile floor beneath the shattered window.
He followed them across the room to the door and
down the hall to a media lab that had been looted
of a television and VCR the night before. Considering
the list of missing items, he stroked his mustache and
scowled at their familiarity.

"Whoever it was," he muttered, heaving a re-
signed sigh before finding a phone to contact a certain parole officer.

*   *   *

"Not me," Arnie Boyd told him, glancing up from his squatting position in front of the candy shelves. Carefully aligning a handful of Hershey bars in the correct box, he smirked. "You won't find any of my fingerprints."

"Arnie. Arnie. You stupid jerk!"

Sinclair held up the denim jacket he had retrieved from a hook in the back of the convenience store and displayed a blood-soaked tear in the right sleeve. "Show me your right arm. Not that one, dummy. The *other* right one."

The deep, scabbed-over scratch near Arnie's elbow matched up neatly with the rip in the sleeve of the jacket. His self-satisfied grin disappeared in confusion as the detective pulled out his handcuffs.

"Come along."

"Cut myself opening boxes," Arnie protested weakly.

"Sure you did. Watch your head."

From the backseat of the squad car, Arnie watched wistfully as the purloined television and VCR and an assortment of secondhand videotapes were carried out of his basement dungeon as evidence. Sinclair came out of the convenience store, counting $38.29 that had been recovered from a Good & Plenty box under Arnie's cot.

"Dammit, Arnie. You just weren't cut out to be a burglar. Can't you get that through your thick skull?"

"But I didn't leave any fingerprints."

Arnie Boyd put in over three years of a five-year sentence at the Hiland Mountain Correctional Center in Eagle River before he was able to return to Anchorage, once again a free man. He had hated being locked up, but admitting it was his own fault, had taken advantage of the situation to learn everything he could about burglary from his fellow inmates. They often gave him conficting advice, but he had come away with some very specific ideas on what might and might not work.

"Forget about schools."

"You gotta protect yourself."

"Never carry a piece."

"Ya gotta have a plan before ya do the place."

"Go for it. Don't pass up a good chance."

"Premeditation will add to the sentence if they catch you."

"There's a lotta rich bastards up on the hillside in Anchorage who take vacations in the winter."

It never crossed Arnie's mind that his instructors probably wouldn't be fellow inmates if they had been successful at the crimes for which they had been incarcerated.

Upon release, he spent a few weeks in a halfway house, picking up highway trash for the city and having long talks with his new parole officer on the virtues of going straight.

It was early December when he finally found a job washing dishes in a midtown Denny's restaurant. His hands were constantly wrinkled and smelled of stale food and detergent, but he got his meals and a little more than minimum wage, so he could pay rent. He moved into a cracker-box apartment of his own that was furnished with another saggy bed, an ancient sofa missing one leg, two chairs, and a surprisingly solid table. The refrigerator's freezer compartment built up ice faster than the stairs outside the place and the stove had only two burners that worked, but, with a towel to stop up the draft that whistled under the front door, it was almost warm and it seemed like home to Arnie.

Going down those outside stairs was a life-threatening, cling-to-the-banister experience, and, once he made it, two feet of snow made walking ten blocks to and from work a discouraging and, at times, terrifying obstacle course. Sidewalks were rare, and those plowed free of snow less than a hope. Though he could make his way across cleared parking lots and side streets for some of the trip, he frequently had to walk along the edge of slippery streets full of cross-town traffic. Narrow lanes and inconsiderate drivers often exacted flailing leaps of magnificent proportions that landed Arnie hip-deep in piles of dirty snow plowed up by street maintenance, cursing some motorist who honked as he passed.

He usually arrived at work chilled and covered with snow that melted into pools at his feet and soaked his jeans. Though he had liberated a decent pair of waterproof boots from the Salvation Army, snow always sifted in over their tops to infuse his socks. The parka from Denny's lost and found had evidently belonged to a careless smoker, for it leaked down feathers from several cigarette burns not patched with duct tape. It grew thinner by the week.

As the December sun rose at approximately 10:00 A.M. morning and set at 4:00 P.M., he was forced to

make his trip from home to work, and vice versa, in
the dark, and evenings seemed endlessly boring. So
it was no wonder that two or three times a week he
struggled a block out of his way to break up the trip
at a local tavern for a beer and a game of pool.

"Your break, Arnie."

Crack!

"Red in the corner. Catch a lift with you in the
morning, Skip?"

"Sorry. Got a job on the slope, so I'm headed
north tomorrow."

"Hey, good for you." Jobs at the Prudhoe Bay oil
field were difficult to get and paid fantasy amounts.

Arnie frowned. His pool partner, who lived
nearby, sometimes gave him a ride to work, but that
was obviously a thing of the past. He nodded at the
blue ball, the side pocket, and leaned to line up the
shot, took it, and missed, his concentration ruined.

"Damn!"

Skip chalked up the tip of his cue and studied the
arrangement of the balls on the table.

"I won't need the car for the next couple of weeks.
Why don't you take it?"

Arnie froze, Budweiser bottle almost to his lips,
and rolled his eyes in the direction of this astonishing
offer. Just like that, for the price of a little gas, his
problem solved.

"You sure?"

"Yeah. Why not? Drop me off tonight and park it
at your place, okay?"

"You bet! Thanks."

*   *   *

For three days Arnie luxuriated in having transportation. Skip's ancient Mercury had little in the way of
suspension, one fender was rusting through, and the
heater, when it worked at all, was stuck on High,
but Arnie lovingly swept new snow off each morning
and scraped ice from the windshield. He drove to
the grocery and ferried home his meager purchases
in smug comfort. Twice he stopped at the tavern after
work, carefully parking the car where he could look
out a window and see it still there, waiting to carry
him home.

On the third evening, he counted his pocket
change and went directly back to his apartment
where he settled in to read a copy of a newspaper
someone had left at the restaurant. Halfway through
its pages, he came to the daily television schedule
and ran a finger down the listings to see what movies
he was missing. There were two favorites and three
or four he'd like to have seen. He sighed and raised
his eyes to an empty section of wall across the room
where he would have put a television, if he had one.
Maybe, if he cut out the pool games, he could save
enough money to pick up a used set in some pawn-
shop. Flipping on through the paper, he opened to
an advertisement for Hawaiian vacations.

*"There's a lotta rich bastards up on the hillside in An-
chorage who take vacations in the winter,"* he recalled.
But the hillside was miles away and out of reach.

No! It wasn't! He had transportation, he suddenly
realized, and for a moment scarcely breathed at the

thought. He had a car that would take him there and a week and a half before Skip would return to claim his vehicle.

His day off arrived two days later. He walked the floor until it finally grew light in the morning, then drove south of town and up to the streets of big, expensive houses that occupied the bluff below the Chugach Mountains. Their wide windows faced over a hundred miles of the magnificent scenery of Cook Inlet and its surroundings, clear and beautiful in the cold morning light. He stopped at the top for a few minutes, just to appreciate the view of Mount Susitna. There wasn't a breath of wind, and smoke from wood-fires rose in straight lines from chimneys.

Deep purple shadows were beginning to grow long across the snow when, many winding roads later, Arnie finally found what he was looking for—a large, isolated house with an unplowed driveway. He examined it closely as he drove slowly past, but saw no light or smoke. No one had been there in days, maybe even weeks. A small grove of spruce between the place and its nearest neighbor would provide some cover for the tracks he would be forced to make in approaching it. He cruised by it twice more, making sure, then headed back toward midtown, thinking hard.

"Ya gotta have a plan before ya do the place."

Shortly after midnight the next night, he was back—with his plan. Parking the car on the side of the road, he strapped on a borrowed pair of snowshoes over his boots, took a flashlight, several plastic grocery bags, and his new crowbar, and headed off through the grove of spruce trees. From the edge of the trees, he assessed the back of the empty house and was delighted to see that a lower-level patio had been protected by an overhead deck. Quietly crossing the narrow space between house and trees, he was soon standing on this snowless cement space.

Laying down his light and crowbar, he took off his boots, snowshoes still attached, and began to disrobe. Carefully, he took off every stitch of clothing he had on, neatly stacking it in the order he would resume it. Bare-ass, birthday naked, he stood shivering in the cold of the winter night and pulled on a stocking cap and a pair of gloves. Prancing from one bare foot to the other on the chilly cement of the patio, he took a final moment to consider the details of his plan. Everything seemed in order.

No fingerprints or fibers would be left and no window would be broken this time. Approaching the back door, with the crowbar, he pried it open, and waited, listening intently. Hearing no response to the noise, he quickly disappeared into the dark interior of the house, cautiously shielding the beam of the flashlight with his gloved fingers.

Arnie made two trips back through the trees to Skip's car, both of them heavily loaded with electronic equipment and several plastic bags filled with videotapes. The first trip was made hurriedly, muttering four-letter words through his chattering teeth, for he had bothered only to stomp on the boots with snowshoes. Burdened with a large Sony television that obstructed his line of sight, he created a stag-

gered track through the trees as he tried and failed
to keep cold plastic from the cringing flesh of his
naked belly. Before the second trip, however, he
paused long enough to frantically yank clothes back
onto his shivering body, close the back door, and
carry away everything he had brought, along with a
VCR and the bags of videotapes. Before leaving the
area, he pulled the car to the middle of the road,
where other passing vehicles would erase his tire
tracks, and walked back to where it had been parked.
There he used a broom to sweep away any identi-
fying traces of boots or tread.

Heater at full blast, he whistled cheerfully as he
drove down the long hill to the highway and all the
way home—even when he spent the last four dollars
in his pocket for gas at an all-night service station.

The day had been a mixture of sun and late clouds
that loomed up over the Chugach range, threatening
to dump more snow on the city of Anchorage. Detective Will Sinclair stood beside an irate homeowner in
the lower-level family room of a burglarized hillside
house, staring at empty spaces on the shelves of an
entertainment center and watching another technician dust for fingerprints.

"He even took my videos," the woman carped in
disgust.

"Nothing usable here." The technician shook his
head. "I can't find a single print, inside or out—or
anything else, for that matter. Whoever it was made a
hell of a wallow through the trees, but left absolutely
nothing that would identify him."

"Must have left something," Sinclair mused, frowning.

"Not that I can find."

"The door?"

"Nope." He began to pack up his soft brush and black powder.

"No tracks?"

"Huh-uh." The technician shook his head. "Wore snowshoes."

"Tire treads?"

"Smart enough to wipe them out before he left."

Sinclair's scowl deepened in frustration. "There has to be something. Everybody leaves something."

But there seemed to be nothing. Without evidence, there would be no warrant. Without a warrant, there would be no apartment search for the stolen items.

Sinclair was about to admit defeat, when a brilliant ray of late-afternoon sun splashed suddenly into the room. It brightened the space and reflected from the shiny tile floor between Sinclair and the outside door with its broken lock. He squinted in the sudden glare and started to turn away, but something attracted his attention.

Squatting, he directed a hawklike stare along the sunbeam that lit up the tile.

"*Ha!*" He chortled. "Gotcha! Come look at this."

In a straight line from the back door to where the detective crouched, gleefully pointing an index finger, marched the clear, detailed prints of bare feet. Complete with arches, whorls, and loops, each toe-print was individually and identifiably unique.

"Shoulda kept your socks on, Arnie."

AUTHOR'S NOTE:

*The basic essentials of this piece of fiction are based on a
series of real attempts and failures by an actual bungling
burglar. It all happened years ago and was related to me
by John Sauve, retired Certified Latent Examiner for the
Department of Public Safety in Anchorage, Alaska. The
names, personalities, and locations have been changed to
protect the innocent—and the guilty.*

REARRANGEMENTS
Anne Perry

Good Friday, 1964, was a day I shall never forget, for a lot of reasons, good and bad. It was the first anniversary of my mother's death. My two brothers live in the east, but we three sisters, Mary, Jean and I, decided to spend the time together at my home in Seward, Alaska.

I drove over to meet Jean off her flight from Seattle, picking Mary up in Juneau on the way. We were a little on the late side, as is usual where Mary is concerned, because she was busy fetching or carrying for some neighbor or other.

I am the middle sister, Kate—middle in every way, usually at the center of the battles, and the reconciliations, whether I mean to be or not.

Jean was feeling a little emotional, remembering what day it was. She had been the closest to Mother, by a long way, always the favorite, although I don't think she was as aware of that as Mary and I were. It was kind of a sore subject.

For once she forbore from making any criticism about having to stand around the airport for twenty minutes in the cold waiting for us. We greeted her, put her luggage in the trunk of the car, and started back on the long drive, me at the wheel as always. It was my car, and anyway, I hate being driven by anyone else, in fact I won't put up with it. Another thing I won't put up with is Jean's backseat instructions.

We made small talk most of the time, asking about each other's families, especially children. I was divorced, Mary widowed. We both knew and liked Jean's husband, but there was nothing particular to be said about him. As usual there were all the little edges to any remark. We had done it all so often I could have predicted them, but still we went through the motions. Silence would have grown too obvious.

The scenery was magnificent, winding through the razor-edged mountains, still white with snow right down to the shoulders of the road where the traffic had cleared most of it. The valleys opened out and by half past five we were running along the coast road only a couple of miles from home.

All the way Jean had done her usual telling me what to do. I had largely ignored her. I daresay she was only concerned for our safety. Maybe she thought she was helping, but in spite of all my resolutions, it nearly drove me crazy. But since she had done it for the last thirty years, I should not have let it bother me.

"You're going too fast!" she said as I reached a straight stretch.

I said nothing, but increased the pressure of my foot on the gas.

Her voice rose sharply. "You'll hit something!"

"You've got that right!" I snapped back. "And if you tell me one more time how to drive my car, it'll be you!"

"I'm only trying to stop an accident!" she said with great reasonableness.

"It won't be an accident," I retorted. I looked at the speedometer. I wasn't doing more than fifty-five.

"You're too far to the left!" she said with a note of alarm rising to real fear.

I put my foot down further, and the car shot forward and veered into the middle of the road, then right out of my control it went off the other way. It was as if the steering had broken. We went first one way and then slithered back again, all over the road.

I fought with the wheel, wrenching my shoulders in my efforts, and it made no difference at all. I could feel the sweat break out on my body. I was clinging on, fighting it with all my strength, but it was as if the road were fighting back, heaving and twisting under me.

Jean was shrieking. Beside me Mary sat white-knuckled and rigid.

I tried to slow up, but we were still reeling all over the place. The mountains, fields, fences, roadway all swung in front of me, not to mention the better part of my whole life!

"I told you!" Jean yelled. "You're going much too fast!"

I had the brakes on as hard as I dared. We skewed

around crazily, and the next moment there was a terrible jolt and I was thrown forward hard against my seatbelt, and then back again so violently it all but knocked the wind out of me. When I opened my eyes and focused, we were facefirst into the ditch, motionless, the hood buckled and steam rising in a thin, hissing column.

Beside me, Mary was ashen white, but her eyes were open and she seemed to be more or less all right. I swung around to look at Jean the best I could over my shoulder. I was dimly conscious of my knee hurting.

Jean stared back at me, shivering with terror. Then I realized why. We were wedged in the ditch, but everything was still moving! It was shuddering, swaying and jolting all at once, and there was a dull roaring sound that had nothing to do with the engine, which had stopped.

Earthquake! Bigger than anything I'd ever imagined and still going on . . . and on . . . and on! The ground itself was reeling, buckling like a carpet someone had shaken, and odd bits here and there seemed to quiver like boiling oatmeal.

This is an earthquake area, especially close to the sea, so I know something about them. You can get rockfalls, landslides, and infinitely worse than that—tidal waves—great tsunamis that roll in fifteen or twenty feet high—or thirty—or more!

"Get out," I shouted as loudly as I could, trying not to sound hysterical and at the same time feeling for the handle of the door beside me, forcing it open. I could hear Jean scrambling around in the back trying to open her door. "Are we going to catch fire?" Her voice soared in panic.

"No," I answered, with no idea whether that was true or not. "It's an earthquake! Did you think that was just my driving? Thank you very much!" I don't know what made me try to be funny, perhaps to hide from her how scared I was. My vivid imagination already had waves roaring in on us like walls of death. "It'll be okay—just get out!" I yelled. "We need to be away from here. Maybe climb up that ridge inland a bit." I waved my free hand in the general direction of the nearest spur out from the mountains. "Mary! Come on . . . move!"

Mary came to life at last and fumbled for the door handle, finding it and heaving it open about two feet before it got stuck in the earth. She is quite a bit shorter than I am, and definitely more than a bit wider.

"You'll just have to do it!" I said fiercely. "We can't stay here!"

Whether she caught the urgency in my voice, or realized for herself what I was thinking, she threw her weight against it and made not more than an inch or two's difference, but it was enough. She squeezed her body through, gasping and grunting, and landed awkwardly on the snow just as Jean did the same from the back.

"Come on!" Jean called at me impatiently. "If it's going to catch fire, get out! I'll stand here. Someone's bound to come past. We'll get a lift." As she spoke she moved into the middle of the highway just as another violent heave of the ground cracked the tarmac, and a sheet of water shot up eight or ten feet into the air not a dozen yards in front of us.

I think we all screamed. I certainly felt as if I did. I stopped even trying to open my door, and clawed my way across, never mind the gear lever jabbing at me, and fell out of the passenger door, rolled over and stood up. I was bruised and twisted but did that matter? "Get our anoraks," I ordered. "And the blankets and torch out of the trunk."

Mary moved to obey.

The water was still shooting out of the ground, and half a mile ahead there was another geyser like a burst main.

Mary banged the trunk shut, her arms full of clothes, and looked toward the spur of land I'd pointed to.

"We've got to stay here!" Jean told her roughly. "There may not be anybody living up there." She took her anorak from Mary and struggled into it. "I can't see any houses. Anyway, why should they drive us home when someone'll come along any time now. Don't go wandering off, that's just stupid."

I saw Mary's face tighten. For years Jean had been telling her what to do, it's a habit, and for years Mary had been going her own way, building up her temper, but promising one day she'd tell Jean what she thought of her. But family history runs deep. We can't even recall where some of the memories came from: Mary looking after me while Mother was out, which, looking back, seemed to be most of the time, or else she was ill. Me a sickly baby, and stubborn as all get-out. The boys off working as soon as they were old enough. And Jean, generous, funny and spoiled, Mother's favorite, who could do no wrong. Mary promised that one day she'd retaliate, and she never did. And Jean probably never knew she wanted to.

But that was Mary, not me. "It's an earthquake!" I swung around on Jean. "That means there are going to be landslides! Hell! Can't you hear the water sloshing around underneath us now?" I took my anorak too and put it on. It was going to be cold.

Jean swallowed, gulping air. "Then the farther away we are from the hills and any landslides, the better!" she pointed out. "And off the soil. The road's about as firm as anything." She made a move to drag Mary from the shoulder onto the tarmac beside her. "And you!" she said to me sharply.

There was a gurgling, sucking sound, and a pool of water gushed out of what had looked like solid ground a moment ago.

"We're only a hundred yards from the sea," I replied, trying to sound sane and as if I knew what I was talking about, although my heart was going like a trip-hammer. I had not wanted to tell her. Like me, she had a terror of drowning. I don't know where it comes from. "Earthquakes cause tidal waves, Jean."

She stared at me as if I'd spoken to her in Greek.

"Come on," I said more gently. "We've got to get to higher ground; it's not far. We should start moving. It's cold and we'll do a lot better if we stay dry." That was a magnificent understatement. Dry was definitely better than under a twenty foot wall of water. "Come on."

We started to walk, carrying the blanket and torch, and reluctantly, white-faced, Jean caught up with us and we pushed steadily, side by side, up the slope until it became steeper. I was out of breath and so was Mary. I could see her gasping. Only then did I realize how united all three of us were, and for an instant it was as if we were children again, us against the world, and I found myself smiling, all the resentments forgotten.

Mary turned and smiled at me, tears in her eyes.

Then we heard them, loud popping sounds, way over toward the town, and a moment later black smoke billowed against the sky, and then gouts of flame, brilliant yellow and orange.

"What's that?" Jean's voice all but choked in her throat. "Earthquakes don't have lava . . . do they? Oh, God, help us!"

"No!" I said quickly. "No!" I put my arm around her. She was stiff as a tree. "It's the Chevron oil tanks over in Seward. Don't worry, nothing will reach us out here."

"Nothing?" she demanded with a note of hysteria. "What sort of nothing? You mean like fire?"

"Nothing like anything!" I said impatiently. "Except water. Come on, don't stand there, keep moving!"

We started up again, walking more separately now, each looking back at the skyline of the town every now and again as the dark cloud expanded and the flames seemed to get bigger. It was not easy going. The ground was rough, caked in snow in patches, with coarse grass spiking through and we kept slipping. I don't know whether it was clumsiness or fear, or if there were still tremors that threw us off balance.

Over toward the left, water sprayed yards high in the air, up out of a new crack in the earth, and a shower of stones rattled above the slope ahead of us.

Mary plodded on at one side of me, her face set, eyes fixed wide. I wished there was something I could do to reach her, but the invisible barrier between us was as solid as ever. She disapproved of me. She always would. I had run off when I was seventeen. Mother had said I deserted the family and she had never forgiven me for it. I kept on trying to bridge the gulf and finally succeeded, at least a little. We had made some kind of accommodation in the last few years of her life. She had taken back the "disowning" bit, but she had not forgotten it. I had still "betrayed" them all. The price of that was that I could never belong again, even though it was I who sat with Mother at the end when Mary was too hurt and too angry, and Jean was too upset. She had taken Mother's death terribly hard. Unlike for Mary or me, in life nothing had broken the bond between them, and for her the loss was raw and new. I had learned to accept it a while ago and finally Mary had too.

I looked at her now, struggling up the hill beside me in the growing dusk, stubborn, sad, angry with the loneliness inside herself, but still cherishing all the old wounds that I could not reach.

Another oil tank burst with a distant thud and another flame joined the wall of fire. God only knew what was happening to the people over there, but there was nothing we could do to help.

A creek to the right of us roared through a ravine in the rocks, twice its usual size. A loose rock crashed down, bounced, and disappeared, followed by a dozen more.

The ground under my feet gave and suddenly I was in a quagmire up to my ankles, then almost to my knees. I shrieked and Mary froze, then slithered back, holding out her hands toward me. Jean was closer and threw herself onto her stomach as I grasped at her arms, heaving at me for what seemed like an endless time. Every muscle ached and I felt as if my shoulders were coming out of their sockets. Then the next moment we were all three lying in a heap on the shale, sodden wet, shuddering with cold and relief.

"Thank you," I said numbly, and by heaven I meant it.

No one answered.

A few stones bounced and clattered from above us, and rolled down to the grass below.

"I don't know what we're climbing up here for!" Jean said angrily. "You always think you know everything!" That was directed at me. "We should have waited on the road. Someone would have found us! Nobody in their senses is going to look for us here!"

"Nobody's going to be looking for us anywhere," Mary pointed out. "Apart from the fact that they'll all be too busy trying to put the fires out, and attending to burst mains and things like that. And maybe find people trapped under rubble."

She pushed her hands up over her face, unintentionally smearing it with mud. "I wonder how widespread it is? It's possibly hit lots of places. Juneau could be worse than this."

"Or better," I said, trying to comfort her. "Anyway, we're all right. We'll be cold, but we'll survive that." I knew she was thinking of her son and daughters and their families, but there was no way we could find out about them, still less do anything to help.

"We should have stayed by the road!" Jean said yet again. "We . . ." She saw it even before she finished speaking, a wall of water heaving out of the sea, crashing over, roaring toward us, engulfing the land, tearing away trees and sweeping everything in front of it, wild, curling, pale spume-edged in the fading light.

For a moment we were paralyzed.

Then as one we shot to our feet and flung ourselves forward up the incline, scrambling, clawing over every yard of ground as if hell had opened up behind us. My skin was torn and bleeding, nails shredded, clothes ripped before I realized that the wave had broken and stopped short of us. My legs collapsed and I fell into the snow and mud, trying to fill my lungs with the cold air, shuddering and sobbing with relief.

I swiveled around and heard the sucking sound as the water tore the earth away about twenty feet below us, retreating filthy, hungry for debris, grasping after us like a great tongue, then arching back into itself and sliding away again.

The flames on the horizon were brighter. How much oil was there to burn? I had no idea.

"We've got to go higher!" I said, straightening up awkwardly. "The next one could be bigger."

"Why should it be?" Jean demanded. "You're only guessing."

"You want to stay and argue, you do it!" I snapped back at her. She was just perverse enough to stop, and I was afraid she would. It was getting darker and the ground was very rough. Every now and then the earth trembled and more rocks and stones came rattling down. There seemed to be water everywhere, oozing up out of the soil, squelching under our feet, crashing down the hillside in the swollen creek, breaking off chunks of the bank as it went. Nothing was fixed, nothing certain. I put my foot on something, and it gave way, pitching me forward to land on bruised hands and knees.

And there were strange noises, sucking and grinding, as if the earth were gathering its strength for another attempt to throw us off.

Mary was on my left, toiling upward a step at a time, glaring at me occasionally, but never at Jean. This was still the anniversary of Mother's death, and it would take more than an earthquake to cover the rift between them. It was all life deep. Mary could remember the time when Mother and Dad had been happy. Like me, sometimes she had taken Dad's side in the endless fights. For Mother and Jean there was no forgiving that.

On the other side Jean was panting, her face pale in the dying light. She too had never accepted that I had had the right to go. It was my turn to look after things, to stand by my sick mother, and instead I had run off to get married, putting myself first. At least that was how she saw it, and had never let me forget. It wasn't actually spoken of, but it was there underneath the surface, in the little needling remarks.

Sometimes I wondered if I really was as bad as they said. It had seemed to me at the time just a matter of survival. Mother was always going to be ill when she wanted somebody else to do something. She'd been dying every day since I'd been old enough to understand it. She'd been better than ninety when it actually happened. I guess when we talked about our childhood we were like blind men describing an elephant; we each perceived something completely different.

In a way I was as alone struggling up that hill as if there'd been no one else closer than Seward a couple of miles away, burning on the horizon under its pall of smoke, the oil flames still bright.

Then there was another wave, bigger than the last. It came roaring and crashing out of the dusk as if it would never stop. I felt the spray of it sting my face, and its wet, icy breath all around me.

When it retreated we were huddled together on a spur that jutted out over broken scree, and as Jean stood up the ground gave way under her and she teetered for a moment on the edge, her arms waving. Then with a shout of terror she overbalanced and fell flailing over the rim and down, down into the mud, still crying out.

I wasn't prepared for the horror I felt, the engulfing sense of loss, not as if it were my sister who had gone, but a part of me. I went after her without even thinking of how or if I could get back, or even of the next wave!

The ground seemed to cling onto me one moment, and to throw me off the next, but Jean was still below me, and that was all I could think of, all that mattered. Drowning never entered my head.

Mary was beside me, and even without being able to see her face in the gloom, I knew that she felt exactly as I did. For once we acted as one person, scrabbling, pulling and shouting together as we reached Jean and hauled her out of the mud and rubble, talking all the time, nonsense most of it, trying to reassure her, and I suppose ourselves, that she was all right and that we would all get above the waterline before the next wave hit.

We pulled her out, without any help from her, and it was only when we were almost level with the spur that had collapsed that we both realized at the same moment that Jean had not spoken a word, or really moved other than as we had dragged her.

I reached to feel for a pulse at the same moment that Mary did, and our hands collided over Jean's wrist. Was the pulse I felt Jean's or my own? My heart was beating so wildly it could have been either.

"She's alive," Mary said quietly, but there was confidence in it, and I felt myself steadying, breathing more calmly. We sat there together, holding Jean, trying to warm her, to rub a little life back into her arms and hands.

I wanted to say something, to retrieve some of all

that we'd lost, but I didn't know how to begin. I was not sorry for having left all those years ago, but I was sorry for what it had done to Mary and Jean. And I was sorry for the gulf between them that I couldn't help to heal.

"She'll be all right," I said, because I had to believe it.

"I know," Mary replied, but there was more hope in her voice than conviction. "Do you think there'll be another wave?"

I had no idea. "Probably. We'd better be prepared."

Mary smiled at me, I could just make it out in the last of the light.

"I'm sorry I left you," I said suddenly.

She looked surprised, then she shook her head.

"I know you're still angry," I went on hurriedly. "But I paid for it. For half my life I've felt as if I didn't belong, I had no family—and I've missed you!"

Over in the distance, across the floodwater of the last wave, something like a rocket sped over the surface, trailing fire. I nearly missed what Mary said.

"I know you did," her voice was soft in the darkness. "But I still wish I'd made it when I tried. I'm not angry with you, but I'm angry with myself, because I hadn't the guts to do it. I envied you."

There was such honesty in her I couldn't disbelieve it, and yet it astonished me. I'd always thought Mary had all she wanted . . . except Mother's approval, of course. Jean was the only one of us who ever had that.

"You envied me?" I said incredulously, still rubbing Jean's arms with my hands.

Another loose propane gas tank went screaming across the water, spewing fire.

"Yes—but I had nowhere to go," she explained. "I came creeping back, feeling such a failure. But you managed it and you stayed."

I thought of the first few years of happiness, and then all the years afterward when I would have given so much to have had my family back, my sisters. "Too stubborn," I admitted.

She laughed, but it ended in something like a sob. "I'd have called you a liar if you'd said anything else," she answered. "Do you think she'll be all right?" There was fear in her now and she was not trying to hide it anymore. For all the rift between them, she loved Jean, in her own way, and she desperately wanted Jean to love her, to approve of her, just once to say she admired her and that she understood that our world was different from hers, the time when Mother and Dad had been happy, but it was just as real. Jean was not as strong as Mary, not as calm inside with her own belief. There was some hurt in her we'd never been able to reach. Perhaps it hadn't been so easy being the favorite after all.

"Of course she will," I said, forcing myself to believe it. "Rescuers will be out. This is Alaska. We're tough! National disasters are our heritage. And think of all our good Highland ancestors . . ."

She laughed, a trifle hollowly. "Who spent most of our history trying to kill each other."

"Sounds about right," I agreed. "So those of us who made it are pretty tough. Anyway, Jean's too stubborn to give up and die." I knew I should not have said that the moment it was out of my mouth. She wasn't tough and we both knew it. Neither of us wanted to speak of the dreadful time when she had run away, and been found in such deep unhappiness we were afraid she would just will herself dead. We never referred to it, and she never told us what had happened. There are some things too private ever to be touched.

I knew then as I held her limp body in my arms that something in it was still unhealed. All my anger, the rejection, the remembered slights evaporated. They were only words, like spots of blood on the outside. They were not scars, not really, and it was time they were washed off.

There was another wave, screaming out of the darkness, its pale foam hissing, luminous, pink-touched by the fires on the horizon. It curled over and crashed about fifteen feet below us, but I felt the shudder and aftershock of its bruising force. About a mile away I saw more propane tanks whizz by, trailing plumes of flame like rockets.

I'm not sure how long we sat there shivering in silence, even though we were so close we were touching each other. But it was a silence of peace. All kinds of things I had thought I needed to say I now realized that I didn't. We had all traveled the same path in the ways we thought divided us. The differences—Mary's widowhood, Jean's quiet, gentle, frustrating marriage, and my divorce—were not as wildly different either, just turns of events that we could all of us have understood.

Why had we traveled alone when we had not needed to? I should have tried sooner, and much harder. Suddenly I was glad we decided to get together on Mother's anniversary. It was no longer a duty I was performing to try to help Jean, knowing she was the one who would find it most painful.

Anyway, perhaps she wasn't? Maybe Mary was hurting just as much, for the acceptance she would never achieve now. It would be too obvious to thank her in words for all the times she had filled my mother's place when I was a child, but I resolved to let her know some other way.

I don't know how long it was until Jean stirred at last, but I never felt anything that mattered more to me. She coughed and began to move.

Mary tightened her grip. "Jean!" she said urgently. "Are you all right? Don't sit up too quickly. Where do you hurt?"

"Everywhere," Jean said ruefully, but the words didn't matter, it was the strength in her voice and the fact that she was struggling to rise. "What's happened?"

"More waves," I said, but I sounded as if that were a triumph, not a totally predictable disaster. "We're well above them."

She didn't answer, but I felt her relax against me.

We sat close together. I was too cold to sleep, but it was only on the outside. More waves came and went, I didn't count them. We talked now and then, all on the lines of "Do you remember?" But we chose only the good things: picnics—Joe putting a blanket over his head and pretending to be a radio, every time we touched him changing stations and giving us snatches of news, stories, music; skinny-dipping in the creek in the summer; picking wild berries and "borrowing" apples from the neighbors' trees. Mr. Campbell pretended to be mad, but actually he'd have been disappointed if we hadn't tried—and succeeded.

The bitterness was gone. At last we could choose what to remember, and what to let slip away into forgetting.

When dawn came finally, still smudged dark with smoke over the town, we saw the devastation: trees uprooted, land torn away, oil drums and tanks, the shards of buildings, two or three cars strewn over the fields. The water had gone away, leaving mud and debris behind, but the road gleamed like a pale, torn ribbon in the distance, and it was only a matter of climbing down to it and waiting until someone passed. By now all Alaska would know what had happened and there would be people pouring in to help, to search for the lost, to heal the wounds, filled with strength to rebuild.

I wished more than anything else to be part of that.

Good Friday was a day when a lot of things were broken, and Easter was the beginning of things that were better. Mary says the same thing every year, in her own way, and so does Jean.

THE TWIN
Brad Reynolds

Nothing can be said about Coal Porter to make him out as much of a man. But the way he went shouldn't happen to a dog. Porter was a bootlegger and he had a place outside of Bethel that was little more than a shack and was practically hanging over the bank of the Kuskokwim. When he put it up he was probably twenty or thirty feet back, but the river keeps eating the land in big bites and all of a sudden his place was perched right on the edge. So if Coal had stayed around he was going to have to move anyway. And that would have been a major problem because Coal Porter kept his liquor and drugs hidden in a cache beneath the cabin. He had a trapdoor built in the floor boards, and as often as the troopers checked the place out, they never found Coal's stuff. He was real slick that way.

He sold to anyone who had the money. He sold a lot of stuff. To the natives mostly, but there were plenty of white folks in Bethel who knew the shortest way to Coal Porter's place. And if someone was a little short on cash, old Coal was always willing to barter. He'd take your sno-go, your shotgun, or your hat if it was fur, didn't smell, and you offered it in a nice way. He'd trade for just about anything, but what he liked most of all was the Eskimo stuff. That homemade crafted stuff was always good at Coal Porter's. He made a wad of money hauling it into Anchorage and selling it to galleries and tourist stores. There's plenty of folks with shelves of pretty gewgaws that came out from underneath Coal Porter's floor. Lots of natives traded an ivory carving or a grass basket for a quart of cheap booze or a couple of joints, only to spot it in an Anchorage store window three months later, selling for three or four hundred bucks. The one word you never used in Coal's presence was credit. He ran a strictly cash-and-carry business and everyone knew it. But a desperate few prayed he might see the error in his ways and they would occasionally ask for credit. The bootlegger would give a little chuckle and then sic his rottweiler. Coal Porter was a mean weasel and no one liked him much although they sure did like what he had to sell.

Bobby Lincoln and Joe Moses were cousins, both from the same small village: a windblown, fly-specked, mosquito-ridden tundra town about sixty miles downriver from Bethel. The name of the place isn't important for you to know. There's good people still living there who had nothing to do with any of this. Both guys were in their early twenties—old

enough to know better. Or at least you'd think. Neither was very big, but Bobby was the taller of the
two. He wore his hair in a ponytail and he had long,
yellow teeth and that hungry wolf look, which usually means trouble. Joe had short hair and a small,
wiry frame. One of his upper front teeth had a chip
missing and when he smiled it made other people
smile too.

Bobby was definitely the meanest. He'd been on his
own since he was about fourteen, doing pretty much
what he wanted, when he wanted, to whomever he
wanted. He stayed alone in an old cabin at the edge
of the village. No one seems to know much about
his folks. There's some who claim they're living in
Fairbanks and some who say they're in jail. One guy
from that same village claims Bobby ate them both
when he was thirteen. He could have. He had the
teeth for it.

Joe wasn't much better, but he did have family.
He lived at the other end of the village with his twin
sister, Alice, and his grandmother, one of the old-
time Yupiks. The old woman took the two kids when
their parents drowned coming back from Bethel one
spring. She raised them as best she could, which
didn't seem to be all that great. Joe wasn't too bad
unless he was hanging around with his cousin,
Bobby. Unfortunately, he was hanging around Bobby
a lot.

And Bobby was hanging around Alice. A whole
lot. He covered that girl like snow. Never mind that
they were cousins and weren't supposed to be doing

the things they were doing. The old grandmother was deaf as a stone and could sleep through a war, so Bobby and Alice used to wait until she pulled the cloth curtain across her end of the cabin, then they did the nasty while Alice's twin brother put on headphones and kept his eyes fixed mostly on video games. Yes, ma'am, there were mighty cozy times in that cabin. If Grandma wondered why her thin curtain kept fluttering in and out like the bellows on a pump organ, she never asked. She was no fan of Bobby Lincoln's, though. Whenever he came in the cabin she never offered tea or served him any kind of meal. As best she could she tried to ignore him. She kept all her old stuff in boxes at her end of the cabin and never would let Bobby Lincoln anywhere near them. She might have been deaf, but she wasn't blind and she wasn't stupid, either. They say her old man was a shaman—what the people called *angalkuk*—and there are some in the village who claim this woman had twice the smarts and three times the magic her husband ever did. That's one of those stories hard to prove either way. But the point is that everyone knew about Bobby and Alice and everyone knew they were cousins. When you live in a village of less than two hundred, people tend to get a little nervous about cousins getting familiar. You don't want your young folks pissing in the gene pool. But no one was about to tell Bobby Lincoln to keep away from Alice. Not if he ate his parents when he was only thirteen.

Alaska in early March isn't your finest time of year. It's been cold and dark about long enough and by then most of the snow is either black or yellow. Mold on the dry herring is the greenest thing in the village and folks are getting pretty sick of last summer's salmon. To say tempers get a little short is like saying Alaska gets a little cold. If you're going to be stuck in a village anytime in March, you're going to want to be unconscious as much of the time as possible. That's when a guy like Coal Porter becomes the best friend you've ever had. That's also when Coal Porter jacked up his prices about 150 percent. In March, best friends can get pretty expensive. The first eight days of that particular month were about as miserable a time as you can get. It was like Alaska was in reverse, heading back to the Ice Age. There was a hard snow falling straight down, blowing sideways, and coming right up out of the ground. And there was that kind of cold that gets inside your blood and starts to crystallize. Your teeth ache for no reason and your toes curl into hard little knots. March ninth got a little warmer and the tenth was a little better yet. On the eleventh, a few brave souls poked their heads outdoors to see if any mastodons were still around. By the twelfth it got up to minus ten and folks were out in T-shirts, putting up beach umbrellas. In the Moses cabin, Grandma stayed behind her curtain for four days, and Alice was suffering a bad case of mattressback.

That's when Bobby Lincoln decided to ride into Bethel and visit Coal Porter, and he kept slugging Joe in the stomach until he agreed to go along. The trouble was, neither boy had any money. So Bobby came up with this great idea. First he picked a fight

with Alice—something about the way she smelled—
and then he stormed out of there, leaving just the
twins and the old woman in the cabin. He wasn't
gone five minutes before Grandma whipped back her
curtain and stuck her head around, checking to make
sure Bobby was really gone. She grabbed her bar of
soap, her shampoo and towel and headed toward the
steamhouse. That long in a cabin without running
water, in that kind of cold, makes a long, hot steam
feel about as good as two weeks in Hawaii. Bobby
Lincoln was probably right about Alice's smell, but
how could he tell over everybody else's? The girl,
still miffed at her boyfriend, grabbed her own towel
and followed her grandmother. Once the place
cleared out, Joe put the other part of Bobby's plan
into action. He went behind his grandmother's curtain and started rooting around in her boxes. That
part of the cabin was fairly dark, there was only one
window and it was above Grandma's bed. Most of
her cardboard boxes were stacked against the wall.
The top ones were filled with clothes. He found her
yellow, calico *quspeq* lined with squirrel fur but kept
digging. He uncovered an old pair of sealskin muk-
luks, but they had a gamey smell and weren't all that
great so he set them aside. Joe opened another box
and things started getting interesting. This was his
dead grandfather's stuff. There was his sealskin hat
and a pair of fur mittens; both had possibilities. Then
he found a knife with a bone handle. He hit pay dirt
with the next box, digging into old stuff the shaman
used when he made magic in the *qasegiq*, the men's
lodge. Joe felt a little nervous digging through that

kind of stuff, so he didn't look too deep. Near the top of the box there was something wrapped in dark red corduroy and he lifted it out and unwrapped the cloth.

It was a mask. An old Eskimo mask. Joe carried it over to his grandmother's bed and examined it in the thin light coming through the window. It was carved from wood, oblong in shape, and would cover a man's whole face. Stuck in the forehead were three bent and ruffled white feathers, flecked with brown. Joe thought they might be owl. In the center of the mask, two holes were cut for nostrils, and above them, two for eyes. The mouth was a savage, leering gash with an opening big enough to stick your tongue through. The *angalkut* had carved sharp and jagged teeth out of yellowed ivory and stuck them all around the mouth's opening. He had painted the mask ocher, but time and use had softened it to the color of faded brick. There was a band of black that stretched across both eyes, making the face look sort of like a raccoon's. Or a bandit's. In the back there was a leather strap to hold the mask in place.

Shamans were before his time and Joe didn't know a lot about them. But he knew a good *angalkuk* was supposed to have helpers who came out of the spirit world. His grandmother had told him that much. She said a *tuunraq* could either be the spirit of an animal or a human that came back to help the shaman do his work. And she said they could change their appearance, sometimes looking like the bodies of dead people. Her stories used to scare the bejesus out of Joe when he was little. He never knew his grandfather, and after hearing his grandmother's stories, he was kind of glad.

He wrapped the mask back in the corduroy and laid it on the bed, then started cramming the other stuff back into the boxes, restacking them against the wall. He laid the old knife with the bone handle next to the mask. The boxes of clothes he made sure went back on top, the way he found them.

His grandmother and Alice were still in their steam when he left the cabin. Smoke was curling out of the stovepipe poking through the steamhouse roof and he could see the plywood door to the cooling room was pushed half open.

His Arctic Cat was an old one and even in the best of conditions it took some work to start it. After days of sitting out in sub-zero temperatures, the battered snowmachine was acting like it never wanted to run again. But he kept choking and begging and swearing and finally the old thing kicked in. He let it run a minute, then jumped on and headed to Bobby's cabin. He had the knife tucked in his brown coveralls and the mask zipped inside his heavy black parka.

Bobby Lincoln thought his plan was one of the smartest things he ever made up right out of his head. And he figured they could use it over and over. All they had to do was wait for Grandma to leave, then Joe could rummage through her stuff. There were enough cardboard boxes piled in back of that cabin to last them a long, long time. They could probably trade for Coal Porter's whole cache if they wanted. The two boys wasted no time getting out of the village, and their tracks headed in a straight line to Bethel. Bobby let Joe carry the mask, but took the knife for himself. Those boys were thirsty and they ran their engines full out, racing across the frozen tundra like reindeer in heat. They made it to Coal Porter's place in a little over two hours. Both of them and their machines were coated in a sheet of frozen snow and ice. Bobby and Joe were slow getting off; their knees were frozen in position and ice was crusting their eyelids. It took a couple of minutes just to work out the frozen kinks in their bodies. And to finalize their plan. Since Joe had the mask, Bobby decided his cousin should go in and deal with Coal Porter alone. But hold out for the good stuff, Bobby warned him, don't give it away. Like he was a little kid or something.

Joe Moses pushed open the outer door to the cabin but before he went through the second one he unzipped his parka and lifted out the mask. Then he went inside to see the man.

Coal Porter was straddling a broken-backed kitchen chair, his big belly pushing against the table, slurping peaches out of a can. There was a puddle of the sweet, thick syrup on the table below him and rivulets of the same stuff were in his beard and running over his fingers. Coal was not a delicate eater. He had a two-year-old issue of *Playboy* spread out in front of him and he wasn't reading it for the articles. Sitting in the chair across from Coal was the rottweiler, its head bent over the table, licking the last morsels out of a can of Spam. There were no spills beneath the dog. They both looked up when Joe

Moses stumbled in. The dog eyed the young man while Coal Porter fished the last two peaches out of the can. He was still chewing when he finally stood up. Joe unwrapped the mask and held it out in front of him and asked Coal what he could get for it.

Porter looked at the mask in Joe's hand like it might have been something the dog made. But before he reached for it he politely wiped his sticky hands on his jeans. Then he took the mask and hefted it, as if its value was based on its weight. He scowled down at the visage and observed as how it was an ugly old thing. Joe told him his grandfather made it and Coal Porter raised his eyebrows like that impressed him all to heck. He flipped it over and tested the leather strap, then pulled it over his own face, turned around to his dog, and let out a sudden whoop. The rottweiler jumped off its chair and scrambled headfirst under Coal's bed. Only its tail stump showed, and that was squirming a mile a minute. Coal Porter laughed and pulled the mask off his head and said he thought it was probably worth a pint of Jack Daniel's or a fifth of something like vodka. Unless the boy wanted some buds, then he could probably afford a dime bag.

Joe Moses scratched at the side of his hairless chin while he considered Porter's offers. He asked if Coal didn't think he couldn't offer just a little more. Maybe the pint *and* the buds, for instance. Porter didn't think he could. You sure? Joe asked. He was pretty sure, Coal said.

Joe shifted to his other foot and told Porter he'd have to go outside and talk to his cousin. Coal gave him a condescending smile, handed back the mask, and said, you do that. But when you leave the room, he warned, the offer might just have to drop a little lower. He looked around his cabin like there were forty, fifty other people standing in a line. My stuff is going fast, he told the boy.

Bobby Lincoln was not happy standing outside in minus ten degrees. He went around the side and peed against the cabin wall while he waited. When Joe came out and told him what the offer was, he got even less happy. And when his cousin told him the offer might have even dropped lower after he left the cabin, Bobby Lincoln got downright upset. He didn't come racing sixty miles across the tundra to have some fat *gussak* gyp him out of what was rightfully his. That mask was worth a whole case of Jack Daniel's. The longer Bobby stood out there and railed about the white man inside the cabin, the madder he got. Until finally he grabbed the mask out of Joe's hands. Never mind, he said, I'll get it myself. And he pushed against the first door.

Then Bobby Lincoln did a funny thing. Before he charged through that second door he pulled the mask over his face, just like Porter had done. And as he went in, he let out a whoop, just about like Porter's.

Now the thing about a *tuunraq* is that you can't predict what it's going to do unless you're the *angalkuk* and used to dealing with things in the spirit world. Even then, shamans have got to keep a tight rein or the power can get out of hand. Which might account for what happened next in that cabin.

Coal Porter kept a 12-gauge next to his table. But when Bobby Lincoln came in whooping, Coal was on his knees, his front half under the bed, trying to drag his dog out. His butt wiggled when he heard Bobby barging in, but he couldn't get out from under the bed in time. Lincoln had the shaman's old knife out. He hopped right onto the fat man's back and plunged the blade in as deep as it would go. He heard a groan come from underneath the bed and he pulled the knife out and then stabbed again. When Coal Porter's knees buckled beneath him, Bobby jumped off, grabbed the man's legs, and started pulling him out from under the bed. He left the knife still quivering in the man's lower back.

Joe Moses heard the noise and got into the cabin just as Bobby finished pulling Porter from under the bed. He froze in the middle of the floor, his mouth wide open, his eyes about as big as plates. He stood there as his cousin pulled out the knife and struggled to roll the fat man onto his back. Porter was burbling as bright blood started oozing out his mouth and Bobby kicked him in the side of his head. Then he reached down, grabbed a handful of Porter's greasy gray hair and went to work on his throat.

There wasn't anything about Coal Porter to make him much of a man, but the way he went shouldn't happen to a dog. Which may be what that rottweiler was thinking. Or it could have just been the smell of Coal Porter's blood. But that beast suddenly came tearing out from under the bed, not making a sound, and in one leap was across the room and onto Joe

Moses, chomping at his throat and doing a pretty good job of what Bobby was just finishing on Coal Porter.

Joe was down on the floor, his hands grabbing at the dog, trying to pull it away from his throat, but the rottweiler was locked on and grinding away like a glacier on rock. Only a lot faster. And that same bright blood started flecking the stunned and terrorized face of Joe Moses. Bobby left Porter twitching in his own blood and went to help Joe. He kicked at the dog and landed a good one on its ribs, but the rottweiler just scooted away from Bobby, dragging poor Joe like he was a bloody rag doll.

Bobby kicked again but missed. By this time Joe's eyes were rolled to the back of his head and his tongue was lolled out but he was still breathing. Bobby Lincoln tried a couple more kicks but that rottweiler just kept moving away. He finally threw himself onto the dog, slashing it with that bloody knife of his. And then the dog let go of Joe, only it was too late. Bobby slashed and stabbed and beat on that animal until it was lying dead in a pool of blood and fur. The inside of that cabin was a sight.

He could see Joe's chest lifting and falling as he knelt beside him. His cousin's eyes were still back someplace where they didn't belong and his face was drained white. Joe's throat was ripped wide open, and the sounds that were coming out were like winds in a terrible storm. Bobby Lincoln knelt there and watched as his cousin died.

He didn't find Porter's cache, but he didn't look too hard, either. With three bodies and all that blood,

Bobby Lincoln was anxious to be somewhere else. The *tuunraq* mask was lying next to Coal Porter and he carried it over and laid it just above Joe's head. He pushed the knife deep into the dog's side, then wiped his own bloody prints off it and lifted Joe's hand, wrapping his fingers around the bone handle and pressing hard. He did his best to keep his feet out of the pools of blood. When he left, he closed both doors behind him.

Bobby drove his snowmachine into Bethel, losing his trail in the town's streets. When he doubled back he purposely rode over his own tracks going in the other direction. By the time the boy got home, it was dark and he went directly to his own cabin and parked his machine around the side. Once inside, he called the Moses house and when Alice answered he asked to talk to Joe. When Alice said she thought her brother was with him, Bobby said no, he hadn't seen him since that morning. Then Bobby apologized for saying those rude things about the way she smelled. Alice was quiet a minute and then said that was okay because she did, but she and her grandmother had taken a steam and now she smelled pretty good. Maybe Bobby would like to come over and smell her himself and he said maybe he would.

The twins' grandmother was sitting in front of the TV when Bobby Lincoln walked in but when she saw who it was she made a sour face and silently got up and went back to her part of the cabin, closing the thin cloth curtain behind her. Alice grinned and shrugged her shoulders. Bobby asked where was Joe and she said he still wasn't home. Maybe he went hunting, she guessed. It was Bobby's turn to shrug. Alice smelled pretty good and that night Bobby spent a lot of time checking her out. And in the morning, Joe still wasn't home.

The troopers came in about ten o'clock. Bobby and Alice were still under the blankets so they asked the two men in uniform to please step back outside until they were decent. When they came back in, the grandmother emerged from behind her curtain and they all sat down and heard the bad news. The troopers said they were still investigating at Porter's cabin, but it looked like Joe and Coal got into it and then the dog, too. They had found the trapdoor to Coal's cache from the blood that seeped into the floor's seams and they thought Joe was probably bartering for some of Coal's stuff. Joe had a mask he was trying to trade, the troopers explained. The grandmother's eyes clouded over and she shrunk down inside her *quspeq* and didn't lift her head up after that.

Alice was crying hard because this was her twin brother and now she and her grandmother were alone, and Bobby Lincoln wrapped his arm protectively around her shoulders and assured her he was there for her. The troopers told Alice they would keep her informed and then they left. She cried some more and Bobby held her tight. The grandmother got off her chair and went to the back of the cabin and pulled her curtain closed. Bobby did his best to comfort Alice and he never went far from her side the rest of the day.

That night they were watching *Wheel of Fortune* when Bobby Lincoln felt the hairs on the back of his neck rise straight up and begin to twitch. He looked back over his shoulder toward the curtain, thinking Grandma might be sneaking up on him with an axe, but her curtain was still pulled and there was no sign of the old woman. When he turned back around he caught some movement from the window in the kitchen and when he looked, there was Joe Moses, wearing the mask, looking in at him. Bobby let loose an awful yell, scaring poor Alice so bad she slid to the floor. He leaped off the couch and out the front door, racing around to the side of the house. Only Joe wasn't there. He went clear around until he reached the front door, then circled the house again, just to make sure. Joe wasn't there. A badly shaken Bobby Lincoln went back inside. Alice was off the floor by now, demanding an explanation, so Bobby told her he thought he saw someone at the window, only he didn't say he thought it was her twin. He kept that part to himself.

Watching television with Alice Moses was not quite as relaxing after that. Bobby kept squirming around, looking back at the window and finally Alice said fine, if he wasn't going to sit still, she was going to bed. She went back to check on her grandmother and say goodnight, then she crawled into her bed. Bobby watched as she undressed and then he joined her.

*   *   *

A wind blew up sometime around midnight and whistled around the cabin walls. Bobby woke up when it first started but recognizing the sound, rolled over and went back to sleep. Along around two A.M. there was a light tapping, as if a tree limb was knocking against one of the windowpanes. But in the Yukon-Kuskokwim Delta there are no trees, so this was an unusual sound and Bobby Lincoln woke a second time. When he looked for what was making the noise, there was Joe Moses in that mask again, looking right at him through the window, tapping his finger on the glass. They stared at each other for a few seconds, then Joe disappeared and Bobby got out of Alice's bed and went over to the window. There was nothing out there that he could see and if he wasn't naked he might have gone out to look. He was already shivering pretty bad and it wasn't from the cold. He got dressed and sat on the couch, waiting, but Joe never came back.

The next morning Alice's grandmother came out from behind her curtain, even though Bobby was still in the house. The laws of nature were stronger than her dislike for the boy, and nature was demanding she use the honey bucket. They kept it in a little porch off the side of the house, where the odor wouldn't drift back inside. Alice fixed her tea and toast while Grandma was gone and had it waiting on the table when she came back. The old woman looked over at Bobby, still sitting on the couch, and walked right past the table and into the back of the cabin, pulling the curtain firmly closed behind her. Alice picked up the tea and toast and followed her behind the curtain. There was no use arguing with the old girl so Alice sat on the bed next to her grandmother while she ate, then carried the empty cup and dirty plate back out to the sink.

You need to move down to my place, Bobby told her when she finished washing the breakfast dishes. But Alice said no, her grandmother needed her and she was staying there. Bobby left then and didn't come back until dinnertime.

The two of them sat at the table and ate caribou stew while they listened to Alice's grandmother eating hers on the bed behind the curtain. They could hear the old woman's spoon as it scraped against the bottom of her bowl and then Alice went back and carried the empty dish out to the sink. They watched TV again, but Bobby was waiting for Joe to reappear and neither one of them ever got too relaxed. About eleven o'clock, Alice went to bed and Bobby went to use the honey bucket. He was sitting out there in the dark, with his pants around his ankles, when the door suddenly flew back, slamming hard against the side. Joe Moses had on a thick, black snowsuit zipped up to his neck and he was still wearing that damn mask. This time he had a hatchet in his right hand and as Bobby started to lean down to grab his pants, Joe swung hard and buried the blade in the floor, right between Bobby's feet. If that boy could have squeezed down the honey bucket, he would have dived right in. He let loose a loud, high-pitched scream, which brought Alice running from the house wearing only a parka over her flannel nightgown. But by the time she got there her twin had already disappeared and all she saw was her boyfriend sit-

ting there with his pants down, blubbering like a
baby. And he kept crying as she helped him back
into the house. They were both shivering when they
came in and Alice's grandmother had her head
poked around the curtain, watching as they shuffled
over to the couch. Alice fixed him tea while Bobby
sat there, still shaking. Then she cuddled up beside
him and made him tell what happened.

First he told her about seeing Joe in the window
the night before, and how he came back and tapped
on the glass in the middle of the night. Alice put her
hand to her mouth and her eyes grew large and
round but she kept quiet and let him finish. Then he
told her about sitting on the honey bucket and Joe
yanking open the door and swinging at him with the
hatchet. He said he could see Joe's eyes through the
mask and they were shining like two red-hot coals.
He thought he might have heard him let out a
ghostly groan, too. When he was done, Alice asked
why her brother would have swung at him with a
hatchet. Bobby took a moment to think about that
and then said he didn't really know. He and Joe were
pretty good friends, he thought, but now that he was
a ghost it was a little hard to figure out what his
cousin might be thinking. Bobby didn't say anything
about his participation in the events at Coal Porter's.
He could see Alice was already upset about her twin
being a ghost and he thought it best not to upset her
any more than she already was. But then he did remind her that a *tuunraq* mask was supposed to have
a lot of powers, and maybe it was making Joe's ghost
do creepy things.

In all the time Alice lived with her grandmother, she had never asked much about her grandfather being a shaman. That seemed to be something her grandmother did not want to talk about about. Shamans were part of the old ways, and most of those were gone and long forgotten. There was still plenty that was magical in the village, but now it was television with movie channels and Internet connections and microwaved popcorn. Magic doesn't necessarily go away, it just changes its appearance. Sort of like a *tuunraq*. But if Joe's ghost was upset, they were going to have to find some way to calm it down. Maybe, Alice said thoughtfully, things might get better once they buried his body. Bobby said he wasn't sure he could wait that long, especially if Joe was going to keep doing things with a hatchet. Tapping on a window was one thing, but attacking a man when his pants were down was something else. He intended no offense to Alice, he said, but her twin had already killed Coal Porter for no reason anyone knew about. Now it looked like he was coming after his best friend.

Alice did take some offense to that. When someone has just called your twin brother a murderer, it's hard to keep feeling warm and cozy toward him. She looked over at Bobby Lincoln a moment and then suggested maybe he would feel safer if he stayed in his own house for awhile. Maybe the reason her brother was upset was because Bobby seemed to be around all the time, eating their food and sleeping in her bed and not really doing much of anything to help out around the place. And Grandma was forced to take up permanent residence behind the curtain now, and maybe Joe was upset about that, too. Alice said that Joe might feel better about things if Bobby Lincoln slept in his own bed for a change. That cabin started feeling real chilly all of a sudden, as if the outside door had been left wide open or Joe's cold ghost was suddenly inside. Bobby's eyes narrowed into two small slits. He stood up from the couch and said yeah, maybe that wasn't such a bad idea Alice had. He always knew she cared more about that old woman than she did about him. And sleeping in her bed wasn't all that much fun right now. Maybe you're right, he said, tightening both his hands into fists. He started to step toward her when there was a loud knock from the side of the cabin. Bobby swung on his heel and ran to the window, peering out at the darkness. But if Joe was out there, he never saw him. Alice had stood up and moved over by the kitchen table and when Bobby turned back around he just looked at her standing there. Then he picked up his parka and pulled it on and stomped out the door, not even bothering to pull it shut behind him. Alice waited until she heard his snowmachine drive off, then she closed the door and locked it, climbed back into her bed, and cried herself to sleep.

The next morning, when Alice awoke, the curtain was pulled back and her grandmother was sitting at the kitchen table, sipping tea and watching her as she stirred in her bed. The old woman smiled softly and quietly wished her good morning. Alice smiled back.

The two women spent that day together, cleaning out the cabin and putting Joe's things off to one side. Alice came across a pair of Bobby Lincoln's boxer shorts and one of his sweatshirts and she folded them into a paper bag and set it next to the door. In the afternoon Alice and her grandmother baked bread and when one of them knocked the flour sack onto the floor they both giggled like little girls. Bobby did not come around, but neither did Joe or his ghost. There was bingo in the community hall that night and they both went and Alice won twenty dollars. Bobby Lincoln was not at bingo either.

He was still brooding about his argument with Alice. He had just about convinced himself that Joe Moses really was responsible for Coal Porter's death, and he was feeling righteously abused by Joe's ghost. And also a little scared. So going up to Alice's was not much of a temptation and he never even thought about going to bingo. Once it got dark, Bobby hung clothes over his windows and tried to ignore all the little night noises that he ordinarily never heard. He waited until after midnight to go to bed and he had a hard time falling to sleep.

Shortly after he did, he was awakened. The clothing he hung so carefully over his windows was on the floor and his small cabin was filled with moonlight. He could see someone moving in the far corner and then Joe Moses crossed the room and stood over his bed, looking down at him. Bobby could not cry out or move or do anything but stare up at the masked figure hovering over him.

He was blinded by the blood. He never saw Joe
throw it, but there must have been about a cup full
and suddenly his face was drenched in blood and
his nostrils filled with the sharp, earthy stench. He
grabbed blindly for his sheet, swiping at his eyes,
trying to clear them. By the time he could see again,
Joe was gone and there was moonlight pouring in
through the open door. Bobby jumped out of bed
and dressed himself, pulling on his parka and boots.
He grabbed his mittens and raced out the door,
climbed onto his snowmachine and tore out of town.
In the stillness of the village you could hear his engine over a mile away as Bobby streaked across the
tundra.

The next afternoon he was found by two hunters
about thirty miles due west of the village, curled into
a tight ball, lying in a snowdrift on the frozen tundra.
He was wearing only one of his mittens and there
was still some blood on his face, although it was
frozen now. The hunters lifted his body onto their
sled and followed Bobby's tracks back to his snowmachine, about four miles farther west. Why he took
off like that, in the middle of the night, without first
filling his gas tank, was a puzzle.

After the days of mourning, that village buried
both boys at the same time, side by side. As was the
custom, there was a potlatch in the school gym
afterward.

Alice ended up burning the paper sack with the
boxers and sweatshirt, and she gave most of her
twin's things to the men and boys in the village. A
few days after the burial, with her grandmother's

help, she took down the curtain that divided the cabin. With just the two of them, there was no need for it. They pushed the dresser that used to be Joe's next to grandmother's bed, and Alice helped her unpack the clothes folded into the cardboard boxes. In the third box she opened, Alice found an oblong mask with yellowed ivory teeth set around the mouth hole and a band of black painted across the eyes. She carried it over to the window above her grandmother's bed and studied it in the light. The old woman watched her. When Alice turned toward her and held out the mask, Grandma lifted her eyebrows. Your grandfather made that, she told her. He made two exactly alike and he used them in the men's lodge sometimes. After you twins were born, Grandma said, he put them away. He did not know all the power in those twin masks and he wanted to wait until you and Joe were grown up. Grandma nodded to the mask in Alice's hands. You can have that one, she said. Your brother took the twin.

TERMINAL
Kim Rich

Michael arrived at the city jail in Fairbanks midmorning. He checked in at the front desk, cleared his credentials, and was led by one of the jail guards into an interrogation room. The room was a windowless, cinderblock affair, painted battleship gray, and containing a single wooden table with a chair on either side. Eddie sat in one of them.

"If it ain't the fucking white sheep of the family!" Eddie said.

Michael said nothing as he sat down in the other chair. Eddie looked bad. Usually did. Like what he was—a junkie in need of a fix. His long, stringy brown hair was matted with sweat against his forehead, his hands shook, and he looked older than Michael, though he was actually three years younger.

Finally, Eddie spoke up. "Man, oh man. You seen Joe yet? Boy, wait 'til he gets a load of you. You haven't changed one bit. You still look like the same straight asshole you always looked like. Man, I can't fucking believe you actually came. Never came before. No. Not ever. Not fucking ever. Not when I got arrested on that trumped-up charge in Reno. Not when Daddy died. Not even when Mama went. Sonuvabitch, and here you are now. So whadaya gotta say for yourself?"

Michael glared at his baby brother. The little bastard was still as cocky as ever. "You really screwed up this time, Eddie."

"I didn't do what they said I did!"

Michael shrugged.

Eddie leaned over the table. "Didn't you hear me, man?"

"I heard what I always hear."

"I know who killed those two men."

"Look, they got you, Eddie. I've seen the file. I talked to the arresting officer. They got an eyewitness who saw your truck in the area where the bodies were found. All they need now is for you to tell them where to find the murder weapon. That's why I'm here, right? To clean this thing up."

Eddie was now out of his chair, waving his arms and whatnot and acting like a damn fool; like he always did when he was in trouble. "They got nothin' man! I've been set up!"

"It's always a set-up with you," Michael shot back.

Eddie leaned in now, real close. "You're still the same old self-righteous sonuvabitch you always were!"

Michael was standing now too, and looking down on Eddie, nose-to-nose. "I got a right to be. I'm not the one wearing leg irons."

Eddie stood his ground. "That's for goddamn sure. You've always made sure of that!"

Michael let out a huff, threw his arms into the air, and walked to the far corner of the room. He stopped, turned, looked back at Eddie. "It was only a matter of time before something like this happened."

Eddie stepped toward him. "Something like what?! Nothin' happened, man!"

That was it. Michael lost it. "I don't want any part of this," he yelled. "I never wanted any part of this, none of it! Not your crap, not Daddy's whoring and gambling, or Joe's! Why can't you all just leave me alone!"

Eddie got that hurt look in his eyes, the one he always got when Michael left him behind on the way to school, or when Michael smashed Eddie's Alvin & the Chipmunks record, or whenever Michael would shove Eddie down on his ass.

No shoving needed now. Eddie collapsed on his own, at the table, his head buried in his arms. Seemed he was crying. "I need you, man. I need you."

Eddie, first-class fuck-up, still knew how to push Michael's buttons. Michael sighed, sat back down, and waited for the tension to leave the room. Real quietlike now. "Why don't you just tell the folks here what they want to know?"

Eddie looked up.

"You gotta get me out of here. I can't talk here, man."

"I don't know," Michael said shaking his head. "Why me? Why'd you send for me?"

"Because you're so fucking honest, man."

"I'm working to get over it."

A minute passed, maybe two. Neither spoke. Then the guard poked his head into the room.

"There's someone else here to see you, Eddie."

Michael stood. Eddie too got up, walked around the corner of the table, and grabbed Michael in a bear hug.

"I'm sorry, man. Sorry about it all," Eddie said, his voice cracking. "I love you."

Eddie was always the sensitive one. Michael got the looks, Joe the brains, and Eddie the heart. That's what their mom used to say.

Michael hugged him back. They stood there like that for a minute. Michael patted Eddie on the shoulders, then eased Eddie away and stepped toward the door. As Michael was about to go out, he looked back at Eddie, whose face was streaked in tears.

"They're going to kill me, you know."

"Who, Eddie? What do you mean?"

Eddie was silent.

Michael turned and walked out.

Eddie's words were still echoing in Michael's head when he walked into the jail's public lobby and came face-to-face with Eddie's other visitor—Joe.

Three years older. Still shaving his head; still wearing a black eye patch. Still happy to remind Michael how he got it. Still bitter. And still with Patty.

She was arm-in-arm with Joe. Patty was part Sioux Indian, and she wore her long black hair as she always did—pulled into a ponytail. Tall, five foot ten. Michael still remembered that. Dressed in pressed blue jeans, a white blouse, and beige leather cowboy boots. She was put together nice, like always.

In high school, it was the same. Of course she was a cheerleader. Prom queen. She came from a nice family. Her dad was in real estate. Mom, the one with the Indian blood, pitched in around the office, but mostly stayed at home to care for Patty and her two older brothers. One became a Jesuit priest. That's what Michael heard.

There was Patty, looking no different from when he last saw her, seven years ago. Then and now, she was the most beautiful woman Michael had ever seen. At that moment, Michael realized that his soon-to-be ex-wife—who had walked out on him just yesterday as he was packing to come to Fairbanks—was right. She'd said Michael didn't love her. True. He was still in love with Patty.

Joe and Michael regarded each other in silence.

"If it ain't Dudley Fucking-Do-Right," Joe finally said, glaring at Michael.

"Hello, Joe." Michael extended his hand. Joe ignored it.

"What are you doing here?" Joe asked.

"This wasn't my idea—"

" 'Course not. Never is. Let me guess, you're here doing your job."

Joe took a step toward Michael, making like he was going to slug him. Michael didn't flinch. Patty stepped between them, gently pulling Joe back.

"Joe, please . . ."

"Please what?!" Joe said, his voice rising, now stepping in front of Patty and holding her away at

arm's length. " 'Please, he's your brother, Joe. You
should forgive him, Joe. It wasn't his fault, he didn't
mean to have you arrested and have the crap beat
out of you—' "

"Joe! Stop!" Patty screamed. People passing by
were looking at them now. Joe paused, still staring
at Michael. Michael stared back. Just like always.

Patty tugged at Joe's arm.

"Let's not do this now," Patty continued, her voice
softening. "Not now."

Joe turned and looked at Patty, then back to
Michael.

"Why don't you just get the fuck out of here? Go
back to fucking Montana, or wherever the fuck it is
you're living these days. You're not welcome here."

He turned as if to leave, then suddenly, Joe gently
pushed Patty aside, whipped around, and hammered
Michael with a powerful left hook. His fist slammed
into Michael's cheek, sending Michael reeling back-
ward. Patty screamed, but before she could do anything, Joe hit Michael again, this time throwing
Michael flat onto his ass.

A couple of officers came around the corner and
pulled Joe back. He shook them off, took one last
look at Michael, then reached for Patty's arm, and
walked briskly away.

One of the officers offered to help Michael up. But
Michael just lay there, watching Joe and Patty go and
wondering if Patty ever thought of him.

That night, Michael got supper at a downtown diner
and went back to his hotel room to keep company

with a six-pack of Miller. He had one beer and fell asleep on the couch with his clothes on. Johnny Carson was on the TV, doing his monologue, some joke about President Ford's clumsiness, when the phone rang.

"Michael?" Patty asked, her voice sounding strained. "Eddie's dead."

Michael sat up and rubbed the sleep from his eyes. He tried to focus on the news, not Patty's voice. It was husky and low, and it sounded like she'd been crying.

"What happened?"

"After we saw you at the jail, Joe got Eddie released on bail. He was supposed to stay with us, but Eddie wanted to go to his apartment and get his things. Joe was supposed to go along, but he got called away to one of his gambling houses. They agreed to meet later at the house, but Eddie never showed up. Finally, Joe went to Eddie's place, and omigod . . ."

Her voice trailed off as she began to cry. Michael stood and went to the window and stared out. He was eight stories up. Directly below, a pair of drunks stumbled across a parking lot. He cracked the window to let in some air. He could hear some guys whooping it up somewhere else downtown, probably coming out of the Mecca bar. On the roof he could see a tattered blue and gold Alaska flag, with its gold stars in the shape of the Big Dipper, flapping in the breeze.

He looked over at the TV and realized he'd already heard the Ford joke, two weeks earlier. He'd forgotten about how network programming aired two weeks later in Alaska. The delay had something to do with shipping the tapes to Hawaii first. Michael felt like he'd jumped back in time. In fact, the whole trip was beginning to feel like one big déjà vu. He felt like he needed some sleep, he felt like he could listen to Patty's voice all night, but mostly he felt stunned by the news of Eddie's death.

"They killed him, Michael," Patty said. "They killed him."

"Where's Joe?"

"At the funeral home." Her tone changed then, more urgent. "Michael, you gotta do something. You gotta find out who did this to Eddie."

"Let me see what I can find out," Michael said, and hung up. He grabbed his coat, turned off the TV, and headed out the door for the police station. No sleep tonight.

The sergeant on duty let Michael read the responding officer's report. The landlady had found Eddie about 9 P.M. when she stopped by to ask about the rent. The front door to his apartment was open; she walked in and found him sprawled in the middle of the living room. He'd OD'd on a combination of heroin and cocaine. He'd bled so profusely from his nose that the walls to his apartment were covered with streaks of blood as his body convulsed and whipped around the apartment's small living room.

He had the music on so loud that none of the neighbors heard anything. They wouldn't have any-

way since the thirteen studio apartments were mostly
rented by Pipeline workers, and most were out in
the field. The body was taken to the funeral home.
Some detective in homicide was handling the final
report. Michael paid him a visit first thing the next
morning.

"This case is closed," said Detective Ron Waters
as he shuffled some papers on the desk.

Michael checked him out. Looked to be about
thirty-five. Paunchy. Probably spent a lot of time behind the desk doing paperwork. Half the job was
paperwork. Michael understood Waters's desire to
wrap up his investigation, but still he had to ask.

"That's it?"

"Look, I know he's your brother. I'm not sure how
I'd react if the same thing happened to me. But we've
been over this. Your brother Eddie was working out
of the union warehouse. He and the other two guys
were running stolen property out of there. Looks like
they had a falling out. My theory is this: Eddie got
rid of the other two—Tom Peterson and Jake Ham-
mond—when he thought they were double-crossing
him. Poor sonuvabitch Eddie couldn't stay off the
dope long enough to go to trial where a jury was
sure as hell going to convict him and throw his ass
in jail for the rest of his life."

"But don't you think it a little strange that bail
was set? C'mon, he was being held on a double
homicide."

"Where you going with this, Leary? I know about
your reputation from when you worked for the de-

partment here; you being a big hero in 'Nam and all. Your Congressional Medal of Honor—"

"Silver Star, actually."

Waters gave Michael a look.

"It was a Silver Star," Michael said.

"Medal, Star, what's the difference, my point is . . ."

"More lives lost, or saved, depending on how you look at it."

"Whatever." Waters sighed. "Bail was set because we got these goddamn liberal judges making all this noise about police brutality, prison reform, prisoner rehabilitation. Like we gotta start feedin' the bastards lobster and shit. Eddie's bail was set at a hundred grand, for Chrissakes. Highest ever been set around these parts. So there ain't nothing goin' on. This deal is as straightforward as they get. It wasn't my idea to bring you up here in the first place. The chief wanted this case solved and Eddie asked for you before he would agree to give us a statement. But now he's dead and it's over. Sorry."

"There's something about this whole thing I don't like."

"Yeah? Well there's a lot of things I don't like. For starters, I don't like your family, never have. I don't like them bringing in Outside uniforms on my watch. No offense. And I don't like that goddamn Jimmy Callahan. He runs the union, he runs that damned Pipeline project. Hell, he owns everybody in this goddamn state. If you don't like the deal, go talk to him. I'm backlogged six months. I don't have the time."

Michael got up and walked out. Here was this Waters fellow, who had joined the department after Michael left Fairbanks, telling Michael what was what. Michael didn't need his thanks, his condolences, and he especially didn't need a lecture. He needed answers and about the last place he expected to get any was from the cops. The kind of information he needed could come from only one place.

"I told Eddie not to be messin' around with those dudes, man," Little Al said as he walked down the length of the bar and brought Michael his drink.

He plopped it down and kept talking. "I mean, what the hell was he thinkin'? Stealing' shit from the union. Those are some bad motherfuckers over there."

Michael was sitting in Al's bar, a strip club called Le Pussycat, which sat on a dirt road, not far from the airport—outside the city limits and beyond the reach of city laws that forbade topless and bottomless dancing.

Little Al wasn't so little, at least not anymore. He stood about five foot ten and weighed about 250. He was wearing a tie-dyed T-shirt, a pair of black sweats, and shoulder-length hair in a ponytail. Business was brisk. About three dozen men filled the bar. A handful of especially sorry-looking types sat at the edge of the dance stage. A trio of dancers, off-shift, worked the floor. It was the middle of the day.

"Nice name, eh?" Al said gesturing toward the neon sign that hung above the bar's tiny stage. "Thought of the name myself. Frenchlike, you know.

And this ain't no cheap whorehouse either. We're a class joint. Got dancers from all over the world coming in here."

The proud owner. "So, what do you think?"

Michael looked down at his drink, a Singapore Sling, replete with a bright pink umbrella, a pink swizzle stick, and a plastic skewer loaded with chunks of pineapple and orange wedges. "What, no flames?"

"Not the drink, man," Al said, pointing toward the stage. "What do you think of Tequila, the dancer? She's my best girl."

Michael looked toward the stage where a petite, dark-skinned dancer wearing nothing at all gyrated to Steppenwolf's "Born to be Wild." She looked wild all right, and stoned, too.

"What about Bourbon? Scotch-n-Water?" Michael said.

Al let out a little snort. "Funny, man. Still the funny man." He shook his head and went to the sink and began washing glasses. "Like I was sayin', this is a class joint. Next week I'm bringing in this Vegas act, Big Bertha and her twin 44's, and I ain't talkin' guns either. Ever hear of her, or them?"

Michael shook his head no.

"She can twist beer bottle caps off with her tits."

Michael raised his eyebrow. "Yeah? How is she with pull tabs?"

"Ha, ha. What do you know? You've been living in goddamn boring Montana working with the Montana Highway Patrol. Shit, man."

Al began pulling some beers from the refrigerator

as a waitress, dressed in a tank top and a denim mini-skirt that barely covered her ass, shouted in an order. A tattoo on her right upper arm read NO-BODY'S ANGEL.

He handed over the beers, then turned to Michael. "Hey, so what are the three biggest lies in Montana?" Michael tried to interrupt, but Al kept on going. "I gave up chewing tobacco last week." "I own this pickup." "I was only helping that sheep over the fence!"

Michael took a sip from his drink. "Heard it."

"Shit, man. I bet you have."

Michael shifted on his stool. "So, back to what you were saying about Eddie and the union warehouse. What's the deal now with that place, anyway?"

"You mean the Terminal? Like you didn't see the billboards all over town—the ones talkin' about 'The I.T.U.'—building Alaska's future and all that shit. I.T.U., man, that's the International Truckers Union. And right now, they own this fuckin' place."

"The I.T.U.?"

"Yeah, man. The I.T.U. is the main source of workers and materials for that damned Pipeline. I know you been in Montana, but you don't tell me you gone stupid on me now. You been there, right, or seen it?"

Actually Michael had. On the way in from the airport, the cabbie drove past the Far North Terminals and gave Michael the rundown on the infamous industrial park, home to a half-dozen gigantic warehouses encircled by a tall chain-link fence. The cabbie and Al told similar stories.

"That place is always going, twenty-four hours a day, seven days a week," Al continued. "They tell me everything's going through there. D-9 Cats and porno magazines. Hell, they got this black market going on where guys are sellin' stuff they're liftin' off the warehouse shelves. I had some asshole in here the other day tryin' to sell me a case of bananas. Like what the fuck am I going to do with a case of bananas? That's what Eddie and one of those other guys was doin'—running stolen shit out there, man. You name it. Trucks, cigarettes, booze."

"Trucks?" Michael asked. "How the hell do you steal, much less fence, something that big?"

Al was at the other end of the bar, prepping another drink order. This one looked to be someone's breakfast—a tall Bloody Mary. Al handed it off to one of the waitresses and rang up the tab before returning to Michael.

He leaned over the bar. Whispering now. "Easy, man. You lose the invoice."

"Lose the invoice?"

"Yeah. Where you been? Thing comes in. Before anybody official-like knows it's there, you drive it out the back door and say it never came."

"That won't work. Whoever shipped it knows it should have arrived."

"Not when three, four dozen of these things are arriving at the same time. Who's counting? Besides, this Pipline deal is a cost-plus operation. It's cheaper to order up a new one than spend time trying to find the one that's missing."

"That's what Eddie was doing?"

Al shook his head. "Oh, yeah. And more."

"What about Joe?"

"What about him?"

"He in on this?"

"Hell no. He and Eddie didn't get along. They had some falling-out a while ago and Joe pretty much stuck to his deal, the gambling parlors. Eddie had his own thing going."

"Do you know what happened between them?"

"Shit, man, they're your brothers."

Michael absentmindedly played with the wedges of fruit in his drink. "We're not close."

"No kidding." Al smirked as he moved down the bar to take another drink order. "The only mystery in this whole deal was what the hell was that Tom Peterson doing messin' 'round with Eddie and Jake. I mean, Jake was some biker badass from Nevada. But that Tom fellow, ain't nobody ever heard of him. Seems he was some Mormon guy from Utah. I heard he has five kids. His widow is staying over at the Higgins Hotel. Apparently this was all a shock to her, hearing her husband was involved in all that crap."

Al delivered the beers, rang the tab, and took another order from another waitress, this one real skinny and wearing only a large T-shirt.

"What hotel did you say she was at again?" Michael asked when Al finished up.

"The Higgins. New place that just opened up."

Michael finished his drink and shoved the empty glass forward.

"Thanks. That was great, but I better get going."

"So, you seen Patty yet?"

Michael didn't answer. Al didn't give up.

"Tough deal, eh? Her marrying Joe and all."

"I left, remember? A little thing called the Vietnam War."

"Hey, don't get all self-righteous on me now. I did my time, too," Al said, now waving his hand. "Ah, what the hell. I'd probably leave town too if I'd put my own brother behind bars. Maybe even enlist, like you."

Michael raised an eyebrow. "Is there something you want to know, Al?"

"Just wondering."

"What, are you a shrink now?"

"I don't know, you O'Learys got the damnedest history."

"It's just Leary now, with an 'L.' "

"Huh?"

"I dropped the 'O.' "

"Excuse me, Mr. Leary with an 'L.' "

Al laughed. So did Michael, who swung around on his bar stool and stood up.

"Thanks. I'll see you later."

Al nodded. "You come back any time. Drinks are on the house. By the way, if you're headed to the warehouse, ask Callahan if I can get a deal on some booze."

As Michael headed for the door, the skinny waitress took the stage. The Rolling Stones's "Sympathy for the Devil" blared from the speakers.

Michael left and was going to see the Peterson widow, but decided to make another stop first.

"Carole, love of my life, how are you?" he asked leaning over the counter in the basement records room for the Fairbanks Police Department.

The room, lit by a series of overhead fluorescent lights, was occupied by one person. Always had been—Carole, a striking redhead. Trim, hair in an updo, matching blue knit slacks and blouse, smoking; still looked thirty-nine years old and holding. But she was fifty, if a day.

Carole glanced up from her desk in the center of the room.

"I heard you were back," she said. She put her cigarette out and walked over to the counter. "I am so sorry about your brother. What a mess, eh?"

Michael said, "Story of my life."

Carole said, "You could rewrite it."

"You name the day," he said with a wink. "How about this weekend?"

Carole put her head in her hands, leaned in real close now. "I don't know. Let me check with my husband." She smiled, leaning closer still. "So, what do you want, big guy? You've always flirted with a purpose."

"I need the file on the Terminal murders."

"That's easy, all you gotta do is ask."

She reached under the counter and pulled out a clipboard and sign-in sheet and slid it toward Michael. He gingerly pushed it back toward her. He gave her a knowing look.

"No, I mean I need to see it . . ."

"I see."

She nodded, turned, and walked toward a row of

file cabinets beside her desk, talking, as if to no one in particular.

"You know, it's just so hard to keep track of things. They cut my budget, they won't hire me any help . . ."

She yanked a file out of a drawer, brought it over to the counter, and laid it in front of Michael. He picked it up.

"Thank you."

"Don't take that too far away," Carole said, pointing at the file.

"I'll have it back in a few minutes."

He left and took the file outside, around back, in an alley, and read through it. Michael was struck by a couple of things. The lone witness, who claimed to have seen Eddie's truck in the area where the victims were found, was missing.

According to the file, she was a union clerk at the warehouse, up from Idaho, where she'd returned shortly after the killings, leaving no forwarding address or phone number. One of the detectives assigned to the case had tried to find her, but with no luck. Seemed even her family had lost track of her. All the police were left with was her initial statement.

But there was something else that puzzled Michael. The Mormon guy was clean. The cops did a federal criminal check and found nothing on him. Not so much as a parking ticket. The widow said the same.

"Never, not once," asserted Lorene Peterson later that day when Michael went to talk to her. "Speeding, parking, you name it—nothing!"

The Peterson widow was like most Mormon women Michael had met—clear skin, blue eyes, exceptionally pretty. Once, Michael had gone to Utah on a case that involved both the Montana Highway Patrol and the Utah Highway Patrol. Michael never got over how perfect-looking all the women he saw on the streets of Salt Lake City appeared. All scrubbed-face beauties toting small children. All well dressed, looking like that damned Osmond family. All filled with the kind of optimism that only religious fervor can generate, and maybe a life without alcohol and coffee.

Mrs. Peterson was sipping herbal tea and fighting back tears, but mostly losing the battle.

"I don't understand. I don't understand. Tom would never have done the things they say he did. He never so much as drank a cup of coffee in his life. I've known him since we were juniors in high school. We did a mission together in Africa. He was the most devout man I'd ever known. He came up here just so he could save some money and then we were going to move to Provo and open a store. He was a deacon in our church back home . . . look."

She held out a photo of a picture-perfect family. Tom and Lorene were surrounded by their brood. Michael stared at the photo.

"Do you have children?" she asked.

"No, ma'am."

Looking up, Michael asked, "Can you tell me where he was staying?"

"He had a little apartment over on Tenth Street. But I've already moved everything out."

"Do you mind if I just go over there and take a look around?"

She shook her head no. "I'll get you the key."

On the drive over, Michael began to think that maybe Al was right. Maybe Eddie didn't kill those men. Maybe Eddie didn't die the way the police say he did. Maybe something else was going on, but what? There's an old police rule: When things seem too complicated, think simple. Nothing was simple about this case.

One thing was clear, however. Eddie and this Tom Peterson lived in the same building. Michael recognized the address as soon as Mrs. Peterson gave it to him.

He tried the landlady's apartment, just to see what she might know about whether Peterson and Eddie knew each other. But no one was home. He took the stairs up to the third floor, turned down the hall, and headed toward apartment "L," which as it turned out, was right across the hall from Eddie's place.

Michael stood in the hall, eyeing the door to each apartment, trying to make a connection. Surely, they must have met. Perhaps this Peterson wasn't as clean as everybody thought.

Michael turned to go into Peterson's place.

POLICE DO NOT ENTER tape zigzagged across the door. Michael reached around the tape to reveal the letter "L." Apartment L, that's what the Peterson widow had said.

Michael used the key she had given him to unlock

the door, gently peeling back enough of the tape to allow him to enter. The widow was right. The place was empty. Michael walked around, poked his nose in the closets and kitchen cabinets. He even looked in the refrigerator. He was in the kitchen, still looking around when he thought he heard a noise. It sounded like someone in the other room.

"Mrs. Peterson? That you?"

No answer.

Instinctively, Michael drew his gun and leaned back against the wall. He stood there, breathing softly. Listening. A cop would identify himself.

Slowly, Michael slid his back against the wall until he came to the doorway to the living room. He peeked around the corner. No one was there. He stepped out of the kitchen, scanning the room before moving into the bedroom. He checked the bathroom next. But he found nothing and no one. He went back to the living room, where he reholstered his gun.

No leads here, he thought as he headed toward the door. He stepped into the hall, and as he was shutting the door, he noticed something curious. The metal letter "L" was missing a screw on the top and evidently when Michael had opened the door to go in, the letter had swung upside-down. He noticed it as he was closing the door. Michael was trying to get it to stay in place when he glanced over at Eddie's door.

A metal letter "I" sat squarely in the middle of Eddie's door. Michael turned back to the letter on Peterson's door. The upside-down scripted "L" looked eerily like the letter "I."

Close counts in horseshoes, but not in mob hits,

Michael thought as he stood looking back and forth between the two doors. He remembered a case he'd read about where some mobsters in Seattle put out a hit on a rival nightclub owner. The hitman sent to do the job knew only that the owner was in the club every night, that he was bald and sat in the same chair at the bar. But what the hitman hadn't counted on was that the owner might be out once in a while and someone, also bald, might sit in the same chair.

Michael shook his head. That "L" and "I" looked an awful lot alike. Things were starting to get simple.

It was late afternoon by the time he arrived at the spot he'd read about in the police report. He parked the rental car along the side of the road and began walking the area.

As he strolled along the ditch, keeping his eyes pinned to the ground, a man drove up on a three-wheeler. He stopped and they introduced themselves. The man's name was Tom Vogler. Michael guessed Vogler to be about sixty-five. He was dressed in wool dress slacks, a Filson woolen jacket, Tuffy boots, and dark brown fedora. The older miners around these parts, when not working, tended to dress well, Michael remembered, as he also noted how Vogler's boots looked freshly polished.

"You live around here?" Michael asked.

"During the summer and fall," Vogler said tugging at the front corner of his hat, pulling it down a bit. "You from around these parts?"

"Used to be. Say, you didn't happen to be around here last week?"

"You mean around the time they found those fellows up on the highway?"

"Yeah."

"You some kind of a cop?"

"Yeah. But that's not why I'm asking. This is personal."

"Uh-huh." Vogler now pushed the brim of his hat back, to get a better look at Michael.

"I don't traffic much with law enforcement types. Got my hands full with the Fish and Game suits. You see I got a placer mine up the road a piece."

Michael looked Vogler in the eye. "Has anybody talked to you?"

"Nope."

"So, you didn't see anything?"

"Didn't say that."

"So, you did see something?"

"Who'd you say you worked for again?"

"I'm with the highway patrol in Montana. My brother was mixed up in that mess."

Tell him the truth, Michael figured. No bullshit.

Vogler cleared his throat, reached into his pocket, yanked out a tin of chewing tobacco, and pulled out a pinch.

"I don't want to be hearing from any local authorities, if you know what I mean. I got enough trouble with 'em." He paused, thinking over what to say next. "I was here the night before they found them men. I was sittin' in my place just back in that patch of woods over there. Havin' dinner when I heard gunshots. By the time I got out to the road, all I saw was some car drive off. I figured it was some city boys out target shootin' or something."

"What about the truck?"

"What truck?"

"You didn't see a white Chevy?"

"No. I said I'd seen a car. One of those what I call land yachts. Looked like a Ford."

Michael thanked Vogler for his time. Climbed back in his car and left and headed back to see Carole to check into any reports of stolen cars. Turned out, a Lincoln Continental had been reported missing from the airport parking lot the day of the shootings. It was a dark blue Lincoln Continental.

"This guy reports it stolen," Carole recounted for Michael. "Guess he got himself looped at the airport bar waiting for his girlfriend, who was coming in on a flight that ended up getting delayed. Next morning, the car was back at the airport. The officer who handled the case figured some teenagers took it out for a joyride. Or the guy was drunker than he thought."

Michael had worked long enough in law enforcement to know that the best place to steal a car is from an airport parking lot. Especially if you only need it for a short time. You run a good chance of picking a car belonging to someone who's out of town and who won't report it missing right away. To get past the pay booth, especially if there's no claim stub in the car, all you gotta do is claim you lost your parking ticket and pay the full day's fare.

Michael thanked Carole once again for her help. He left her office and knew there was only one person he needed to see. The one person whose name kept popping up. The one behind everything; the person he knew there was no point going to until he had all his ducks in a row. Not only were they in a row, they were quacking their damned heads off.

Jimmy Callahan sat silently behind his massive, mahogany, custom-made desk. The desk was big and square looking, like Callahan himself. A crystal and silver-framed mantel clock ticked loudly from the center of an ornately carved buffet next to the fully stocked wet bar. Opposite the bar was a wall of photos.

Michael got past Callahan's secretary no problem. He now stood in Callahan's office, scanning the dozens of framed black and white photographs on the wall. Callahan was in most of them, shaking hands with other men on golf courses, at banquets, in front of worker rallies, warehouses, and with key members of the U.S. Congress, governors, Presidents Kennedy, Johnson, Nixon, and even Ford. Callahan's heft filled photo after photo. His unmistakable broad shoulders, thick black hair, long dark sideburns and square shape were easy to recognize. Except now he was older, in his late sixties.

Michael hadn't even said hello. So Callahan broke the silence first. "Would you like to sit down?"

"No thanks, I'll stand."

"A drink?"

Michael turned to look at Callahan. "No thanks."

Callahan said, "You look like your father. Helluva man."

Michael said, "Been told that," then turned and continued to scan the photos on the wall.

In many of the photos, Callahan wore a sports coat not unlike the one he was wearing now: a yellow, black, and blue plaid. Not loud, but not all that subtle either.

Callahan spoke up again. "Your father was a good businessman. He knew how to keep his customers happy. He knew how to stay ahead of the competition."

Michael turned and stared at Callahan.

Callahan continued. "He knew an opportunity when he saw one. He knew when to get out of the way; how to take a bad situation and make a profit."

Michael turned back to the wall of photographs.

"I think the picture you're looking for is in the far left-hand corner, over there," Callahan said, pointing.

Michael looked in the direction Callahan indicated. He scanned the wall once more until he came to the photo he'd been looking for. In it, two men, ruggedly good looking and in their early twenties, stood side by side on a warehouse dock. Their arms were slung around each other's shoulders, their hips jutting out, in that cocky, we-got-the-world-by-the-balls kind of way. They wore woolen caps, torn dungarees, and cotton work shirts. They looked poor, lean, and hungry. But not unhappy. One of the men was the younger Jimmy Callahan, the other Michael recognized as his own father.

"We started together in Detroit," Callahan said, shifting in his chair. "I got him a job at a warehouse where I was working. The guy was poorer than a church mouse back then. Strong as a fucking ox, though."

Callahan fell silent, then continued. "I don't think I've ever been happier then I was working the docks with your father. He was never much of a working man, though. Spent more time running card games, booze, women, you name it. Even during the war. I guess there wasn't a vice he could resist."

"He didn't kill people."

"That's not a vice," Callahan said, leaning back in his chair. "It's a sin. Besides, he didn't have to."

Michael nodded, not sure what to do or say next.

Suddenly, Callahan tossed his head back and started laughing. Loud and hard, as if he'd just been told the best damn joke he'd ever heard. Michael stared at him, as Callahan laughed so hard, he had to reach for a handkerchief in his pocket to dab the tears welling up in his eyes. What could the bastard find so funny?

"They said you were the kind of cop who'd arrest your own mother—God rest my sister's soul," Callahan said, catching his breath. "So I suppose you'd think nothing of arresting your own uncle. Hell, you arrested your own brother."

Michael glared at Callahan. Callahan took a deep breath, leaned over the desk.

"I know you've been looking into things. I got eyes and ears all over this town."

"So that was one of your boys shadowing me at the Peterson place."

Callahan leaned forward. "You have no idea who or what you're dealing with here, do you?"

"Yes, I do."

"We're building a fucking pyramid!" Callahan said, his voice rising. This goddamn Pipeline . . ." He paused. "Who the fuck do you think you are?" he said, standing. "We're family, for Chrissakes!"

Michael stepped forward. "Leave my family out of this!"

"Your family is in this!"

"Eddie's dead because of you . . ."

"Eddie's dead because he was a fucking idiot!"

"That's why you had him killed?"

"He died because he was stealing from me. Him and that other guy."

"What about Peterson? He was an innocent man."

Michael pulled the metal letter "L" from Peterson's apartment door and slammed it down on Callahan's desk.

Callahan looked it over. Softer now. "He was in the wrong place at the wrong time."

"No doubt, and your hired guns can't read."

Callahan sat back down, sighing. "His widow will live out her days like a queen. His children will all go to college, paid for by the union."

Michael closer now, right up to the edge of the desk. "They'll live out their days without a father."

"Unfortunately, mistakes happen . . ."

Michael leaned in. His face was only inches from Callahan's.

"Mistakes? Your hit men killed an innocent man, framed Eddie, then murdered him too. And all you can say is 'mistakes happen?' "

Callahan rose from his desk and walked to a map

of Alaska on the wall. A red line zigzagged the length of the state, north to south, from Prudhoe Bay to Valdez on Prince William Sound. Across the map colored pins designated Pipeline construction camps. Callahan followed the Pipeline's route with his right forefinger.

"We're right in the middle of this thing. I got thirty thousand men out there at any one time. Do you know how many fucking Troopers they gave me to police things? Thirteen. Thirteen fucking morons to cover eight hundred fucking miles. In one month, I lost twenty-six pieces of heavy machinery. Two were D-9 Cats. Now how the fuck does someone steal a D-9 Cat? I had guys running booze up and down the line. Eddie and that other sonuvabitch were robbing me blind."

"So you had them killed? Eddie was your nephew, for Chrissakes! He was my brother!"

Callahan didn't answer. He turned from the map, walked over to a window, and looked out.

"This Pipeline is a national fucking emergency. It took a goddamn act of Congress to get it done and I got everyone from the President on down breathing down my neck to make sure it happens. I can't afford to have people working against me. Eddie was a miserable fucking junkie. I gave him the job. I covered his ass I don't know how many times. I tried to get him cleaned up. He just wouldn't listen."

Michael backed away from the desk.

"I'm sorry. Peterson was an innocent man. The others, including Eddie, maybe had it coming . . ."

Michael fell silent. What the hell was he going to

say now? The hit men, no doubt some union heat brought in from Outside, were long gone. One witness had already vanished and was possibly even dead. He feared the same would happen to Vogler, the miner he'd met, should Michael reveal what the old miner knew. The local cops didn't have a clue and didn't seem to care. As far as they were concerned, at least two bad apples—Eddie and Jake—were gone from the barrel.

"I know what you're thinking," Callahan said. "But let me tell you any investigation into the union would not be welcomed at any level, within or outside the union. Every congressional district in the country has lines at the gas pump. Any inquiry would slow down construction. No congressman in his right mind is going to let that happen."

Michael stared at Callahan. "I'm going to have to tell the authorities here what I know."

"It's a waste of your time."

"I'll take my chances."

That was it. Callahan didn't say another word. Michael turned and walked out. Went straight to his car. He half expected some goon to catch him in the parking lot. But no one came after him. No one at all, not even Callahan.

Michael got to his car and paused before opening the door. He looked up. He saw Callahan looking down from his top floor view. It was nearly 7 P.M., but the sun was still high. A crisp autumn breeze filled the air. Light, but already growing cool—weather typical for Fairbanks in September. Soon it would be dark and frigid.

Michael thought he might drive out to the grave-yard and visit his parents. Then afterward, well, maybe he'd look up Joe and Patty and tell them what he knew.

He got behind the wheel of the car, started the engine, and drove off. Maybe he'd go see Al. Have a beer at Le Pussycat. See if that what's-her-name and her twin whatevers were in town. Could be worth a look.

GOING HOME

S. J. Rozan

Setting, the sun lays down a golden path across the snow and the water. You could follow it straight to Paradise if you were ready, but you're not: that's for another day. Now, this is enough. The air: sharp, new, and yours alone. The muffled crunch of packed snow under your boots. The silence, vast and complete when you stop. The cold bites but is not bitter; the cold, here, meets you as an equal, and when it fights you it fights fair. The years Outside, the years in New York, you met a different kind of cold: mean, sneaky, the damp its sneering toady as it slipped between your skin and your bones. In New York, snow was gray and thick and betrayed itself into slush and ragged water. In New York, people called you many different names, none of them yours. You lived in run-down rooms, caged above, below, around by other people's rooms, and you ate take-out food, greasy and indistinguishable, off soggy

169

paper plates; but Kenai people know you, Kenai people call you Joe. Here, when you're hungry, you head through the long blue shadows that cut across the golden light, head back toward your cabin, a solid, square black home absolutely alone on the hill. You'll eat trout from the stream that wraps the slope, trout smoked and put by over the brief summer (two fresh, warm months, not the endless, glaring furnace you knew in New York, in those years). This morning, when the light was thin and white, Mom came by, sat and had coffee, left you some pickled beans from last summer's garden; maybe you'll eat them too, absolutely alone, sitting at the window in the spare, empty cabin, watching the ice on the distant river waiting for its chance to find the sea.

"Joe. Joe Craig!"

You look around. Whose voice? There's no one here. You hear knocking. The wind, slapping a shutter against the cabin wall, up on the hill? But the wind is still.

"Anyone in there?"

Your eyes open slowly. With a sadness so deep and soft it almost suffocates you, you know it's happened again. You were dreaming, again. You haven't gone home. You're still Outside: This is New York. This is that rancid room, that stinking summer. The whining fan blows thick, damp air across your sweating face. That's the shrieking of the TV upstairs; there goes the roar of the elevated train. You can hear it but not see it, you can't see anything through the soot-streaked glass but the crumbling brick wall four feet away, the pulled shade on your neighbor's window.

You're still here.

Your heart crashes against your chest, but you tell yourself: Someday. You tell yourself, as you always do: One day, you'll be able to go home. You'll find a way to go back to the emptiness, the vast stillness, where you can be alone, where you can be Joe.

You feel yourself calming; your racing blood slows. Someday. And until then, knowing it's there is enough.

But here, now, who's calling you? The knocking's turned into pounding, pounding on your door. Who is this?

"Open up, Joe. Come on, I know you're in there."

You rise from the bed, glance around at the nothing you have: sagging mattress, sprung couch, yesterday's coffee in a pot on the stove. There isn't anything here that's Joe; it's all another guy, one of those other names. You open the door.

There is a man, shorter than you are, younger, too. He wears a white polo shirt, the underarms darkened with sweat. You don't know him.

"Joe Craig? No, I know you haven't gone by that for a long time now," he says, "but it's Joe Craig, right?"

You shake your head.

"Yeah," he says. "I've been looking for you. Your brother sent me."

"Got no brother," you say.

"Uh-huh. Tom. He wants you to go home."

"This is home." The words almost choke you.

"To Alaska. I'm a private investigator, out of Anchorage. Mick Burke."

He puts out his hand. You reach for it slowly, shake it, tell him, "You got the wrong guy."

"No. Took me six months. That last guy, Lester, you gave him the slip, huh?" He grins.

"Don't know any Lester. What do you want?"

"Look." He holds up a briefcase. "I brought the paperwork. Tom thought maybe you don't believe it." He lifts his eyebrows, looks past you, so you step aside, let him in the room.

He pushes away a crumb-covered plate, a sticky spoon, opens the briefcase on the rickety card table. Back in the cabin, the table is heavy, solid: two thick slabs of fir you set on wide legs, sanded and rubbed and oiled.

The man—Burke, he said—pulls out a folder, starts handing you papers. "They dropped the charges," he's telling you. "That's why Lester came here, if you stayed still long enough to listen. Though I can see why you didn't. Twenty-eight years on the lam, must get to be a habit." He looks at you, right in your eyes.

A shadowy memory, like another dream: a different room, a different stranger.

You say, "You want some other guy."

He taps one of the papers in your hand. It rustles with a sound like dead leaves skidding across the ice. He says it again: "They dropped the charges." He tells you more: "A guy in Idaho, in prison, he was dying. Wanted to clear his conscience. He confessed.

Alaska murder warrant for you's been voided. You can go back any time."

You look at the paper. You think you've seen it before.

He pulls out a file: news clippings. They tell the same story. He looks over your shoulder, points to a date. "A year ago," he says, as though you can't read that. "Couple of months after your mother died. Sorry," he says, seeing your face. "Didn't know if you knew. Lester, he swore up and down he found you, told you the whole thing, but Tom said it was crap. If he told you, you'd have gone back. So Tom hired me." He grins again. He doesn't stop talking. "I started with Lester's report. The way I figured it, Lester located you, but you got wise to him, scrammed before he actually got to you. Right?"

You shake your head again.

He shrugs. "Yeah, whatever. Anyway, Joe, you can go back. And man, that place's changed!" He shakes his head. "It's terrific. I hadn't been down to Kenai in what, twenty years? Until your brother called me. What I remember, it was a real nowhere, more moose than people. But now they got a great road there down from Anchorage, keep it plowed most of the year. Good airport, too. Now it's more tourists than people." He laughs at his own joke. "Houses everywhere, they got a new high school, it's a real town now, Joe. Population's maybe tripled since you left. Hill where your cabin used to be? Tom showed me. Beautiful development, just beautiful, nice big houses, know what I mean?"

You know what he means. The other stranger—
that must have been Lester—told you. You remember
him now, remember that time, in that other room.
He told you a lot of things. The new roads, the new
houses. Fishing licenses now, so many tourists fishing the river. And Mom—what had he said about
Mom? Your head begins to pound.

Burke says, "Your brother, he got a lot for that
land. Lives right in town now. Wants you to go stay
with him. Real convenient, Joe, right near the new
supermarket, the movie theater. Just like you're used
to, all these years here." He grins again, and his teeth
are white, like snow. Sweat crawls down your back.

"Yeah," Burke is saying, "that's how Tom knew
Lester was lying. Lester said he came back the second
day with the plane tickets and you were gone, but
Tom said as much as you loved Kenai, if you knew
you could have gone home you would've, first
chance you got."

Another train rumbles by, screeching as it rounds
the curve. Somewhere close, someone's frying fish,
the smell tossed into your room by the fan. "Christ,
it's hot in here." Burke wipes his forehead, takes out
a cell phone. "Tom said, call him as soon as I found
you." He presses in a number, saying, "You'll really
like it up there, Joe. Place has really changed."

You look at the door, but he's between you and
the door, and he's got the phone against his ear. You
turn, reach into the sink. The knife that's there is
dull, rusted. But it's enough.

It's quick, and after, you pick up the couple of
things you need, step over what you've done, and

leave this room behind, as you've left so many cramped and squalid places. You leave behind the name you used there, too, and take another as you hurry down the baking city streets. Your heart is kicking in your chest but begins to slow again as you think of home. Your cabin, alone on the silent hill. The stream, the ice breaking up, trout running soon, you can fish all day and see no one. Mom will come over, sit at your smooth, heavy table, drinking coffee, laughing. Your skin feels the cold. Your ears are filled with silence. In front of you is a city sidewalk but you don't see that; you see, as you have seen for so long, the hill, the cabin, the golden path and blue shadows. You will see them, and follow them, until the day—and you know it's coming—when you can go home.

THE WORD FOR BREAKING AUGUST SKY

James Sarafin

Tigges stopped the Blazer in front of the hotel and looked across the darkening waters of the Sound to the body floating offshore. He was interested, but not surprised to find a dead man out there. Tigges had been a cop a long time, and the Inupiat Eskimo village of Nuyaqpalik, Alaska, hadn't seen a killing, suicide, or accidental death for almost six months.

He flipped up his parka hood and got out. Rain drummed around his ears as he crossed the street to the narrow gravel beach. Four street lamps in front of the hotel illuminated the beach, and he put their glare behind him. The sheening rain made lines against the dark, seeming to fall in continuous streams instead of drops. The rain lines bent sideways to the wind, saturating his trousers below the parka.

From the high edge of the beach he could see the

clear outline of the body, seeming to float above the waves as it drifted northwest past the long, barren hills that lay across the Sound. Clouds had sunk over the tops of the hills and nearly to the sea, making everything darker than it should have been, in an August evening above the Arctic Circle.

The sound of high-revving boat engines emerged out of the rain. Two open-decked aluminum skiffs rounded the point. They rode high in the water, so neither had made a good catch. One was overtaking the other, with a larger or newer outboard. As they came down the beach opposite Tigges, running close together, he could hear the crews exchanging taunts and curses.

The boat nearest shore went through the floating body right at windshield level. Without any of the men noticing or the boat disturbing the body's course. Now Tigges was surprised: a vision of the dead, distinct from the person who was going to die? He had never seen a simple ghost before.

Gravel crunched behind him, then Charlie Henderson's voice: "The council sent me to see if you found the mayor yet." Tigges hadn't noticed the second vehicle's arrival.

With his back to the streetlights, Henderson's features still showed under his hat. Tigges knew his own face, darker than the Eskimo's, would not show anything beneath his hood—except maybe the gleam of his teeth if he smiled, which he seldom did and wasn't doing now.

"Looks like we just found him." Tigges pointed to the faster boat, which had pulled ahead and was angling toward the beach. One of the men aboard raised his middle finger at the other boat, which continued south, paralleling the shore.

Tigges and his deputy watched the mayor and his crew come ashore. When he'd first come on the job, Tigges had to go find Officer Henderson in the bar. Charlie had been drunk ever since losing his younger brother in a boating accident, for which he blamed himself. Once Tigges managed to sober him up, Henderson turned out to be a good cop and hadn't touched the bottle for over a year.

"The squatters will probably leave soon, since they're not catching much." Tigges gestured at the whitemen's boat, still heading south. At first everyone had thought the salmon were just late, but now it looked like there weren't going to be many at all this year.

Henderson shrugged, worked a stone free with his foot, and sent it tumbling down the steep, narrow beach. "Most of them don't even go out anymore, just hang around camp drinking."

He hadn't seemed to notice the body, floating higher, less substantial than the air. But he had once told Tigges that Inupiats can see ghosts, that he had once seen his own younger brother, trying to talk to him. If Henderson couldn't see this one, it must be Tigges's own vision after all. But who? Always before he had been able to tell who was going to die, and how. And when. When he saw it, death always came soon.

Roger Tigges had seen plenty of the dead flying a transport chopper in Lift Company, Vietnam, '70 and

'71. The dead and the soon-to-be-dead—hauling the one out and the other back in country. On a pickup, when Tigges would drop in fast toward the signal smoke, their bodies leaking blood, flesh and clothing charred by hot metal. Or lying in the paddies where there was no smoke, eyeholes staring into the sky, faces turning black in the sun. Some found with hardly a mark on them, looking as if they had surrendered life without a struggle, had just rolled over quietly in the foxhole or taken time to lay down their arms and sit against a tree to rest.

Then there were the dead who fought for every scrap of their lives being torn away like a sheet, screaming, crying, begging, cursing. Shivering like a fish on the deck, flopping two feet in the air despite medics trying to hold them down.

Sometimes, flying back to base with them stacked three-deep on the deck of his Huey, he heard them through the body bags and over the whine of the turbines, trying to get out, straining to break free even from their lifeless flesh.

After a time the dead and soon-to-be-dead merged in Tigges's mind. He didn't know it until he climbed aboard at base and noticed his door gunner slumped against the open hatch, leaking red from his throat. Tigges grabbed him, trying to staunch the blood, yelling for a medic. But the gunner only pushed him away. "You crazy, man? Let go of me!" Not a mark on him, no sign of blood anymore. Tigges thought he'd hallucinated—until, on return from the mission, enemy fire laced out of the forest canopy. A few rounds clanged into the cabin, a groan came over his headset. He turned and found the gunner slumped dead, just as he'd seen before.

Later he noticed that if he looked right at the troops as they climbed aboard, he could see who was going to be killed and how. The word spread: Don't mess with that black pilot, he looks at you, your number is up. Tigges didn't know when he would see death coming, only knew he couldn't stop it, once seen. No warning had ever worked. He had never found the right words to save someone's life. He only had the future of the dead.

At least here in Nuyaqpalik, he'd found people who believed in the dead.

"Think the council's going to do anything about them?" Henderson was saying.

"Don't know what they can do." The wind gusted a hard burst of rain against Tigges's back. He watched the body, someone's ghost of the future, rise until it disappeared in the clouds. "Why don't you see if the mayor needs a ride to the meeting," he said. "Tell him I'll meet him there, Charlie."

Tigges turned to go back to the late-model Blazer the town had bought with a state grant, still new enough to show it in a place where the roads and weather made a vehicle with 20,000 miles look like it had rolled over the odometer. Halfway across the street, something hit him about what he had just called Officer Henderson.

He turned and said, "Don't take this wrong, but I was wondering: Why do your people use whiteman names?" For Tigges had just been struck by the power of words.

For a moment Henderson made no reply, his face and whole body frozen. He finally responded without looking around.

"I don't know, ask my grandmother. Maybe we don't want them to know our real ones." Then Henderson, still watching the horizon, where the sky showed that unchanging twilight gray of weather turned bad at the end of summer, asked, "Why do yours?"

Tigges drove slowly on the shore road, trying to work out Charlie's meaning. Had he returned Tigges's question seriously, mockingly, or simply to exercise his dry Inupiat humor? In the last two years Charlie had become the closest thing Tigges had to a friend, but sometimes he was no less unfathomable than the rest of his people.

Tigges had gone into police work out of 'Nam, and worked his way up to a lieutenancy in Los Angeles, which most of his colleagues considered a minority promotion. When his wife left him, he drifted north to the Bellevue, Washington, force. Two years later he applied for a job advertised in the newspaper: chief of police for Nuyaqpalik, which on the map looked like one end of the world. All Tigges knew when he accepted the job was that it had no road to anyplace else and that whites were the minority.

Now, taking the long way to the city office, Tigges wished Henderson were sitting in the other seat. At least they had to catch my great-great-whatever-grandmother back in Africa, he imagined himself saying. She didn't take the name in trade, along with some whiteman junk and a bottle of booze. And keep trading on the names for more junk and booze until you've got off-the-chart murder, suicide, and accident rates, in a town with maybe three thousand people in summers when there's work.

He found himself driving faster, the Blazer bouncing hard on the water-hidden ruts. After three days' incessant rain the gravel road no longer made a normal crunching sound, only squishing under the tires. The worn wipers smeared the water, thick, viscous, as if it were oil poured onto the windshield.

As the street narrowed he passed cabins, shacks, and shanties that would have been condemned in any real town, patched and held together with pieces of wood, tin, vinyl sheeting, and anything else that could be nailed together. At least the rain had drowned away the leaking septic smells. Vinyl sheeting and septic systems—more borrowed words for whiteman junk.

A late tour bus from the airport blocked most of the road ahead to let its load of white retirees take pictures, despite the rain and poor light. The big attraction seemed to be the empty fish racks and a caribou hide someone had left hanging over a fence rail to rot in the rain. Through the steamy bus windows, Tigges watched them pointing and gawking, until the driver finally pulled over to let him pass.

When he pulled up to the city office the lights were on in the conference room and the other police Blazer was already parked by the door. He found Charlie reading an old issue of *Scientific American* in the reception area, and sent him home.

They were finishing roll-call as Tigges took a seat. The warmth of the room made his eyes droop as the meeting dragged through various agenda items that might have arisen in any small town. After a time he was brought awake by the anger in the mayor's voice.

"It's the same problem every summer—those damn squatters! They come to town, camp on people's land, dump their trash. The time has come for the city to take a stand. And the chief of police is here tonight to tell us what he can do."

Tigges leaned back in the folding steel chair and looked at the ceiling. They had been through this before, both prior summers of his term. "We got them off private property last year, but now they're on state land. The airport manager says they have as much right there as anyone else, long as they don't interfere with runway operations."

"The airport beach is a cultural site," said another member. "Our ancestors' bones are buried there. The squatters dig up the ground, for their trash and shitpits!"

Tigges started to look, then rolled his eyes back to the ceiling. He didn't like to look at people directly. Never knew who might be dead already, but not know it yet.

"The young people are angry," the mayor said. "Talking about busting up their camp."

"Well, don't encourage them," Tigges replied. "We

haven't had anyone in jail all month, and I'd like to keep it that way."

The council was silent, until the mayor said, "Why can't you arrest the squatters for loitering or something?"

That's what's wrong with this place, Tigges thought. The Eskimos in charge act just like the whiteman. "Because we can't discriminate against nonresidents," he said. "Look, they'll soon be going back upriver to their cabins for the winter. You could pass an emergency ordinance closing bars and liquor stores, just to help things cool down in the meantime."

The whitewoman, wife of the local Presbyterian minister, nodded, but the whiteman and three Inupiats on the council, including the mayor, owned interests in the town's liquor establishments.

"That wouldn't help the local economy," said Briggs, the whiteman. "And it sounds unconstitutional."

"You can do it as a temporary, public safety measure." Tigges almost forgot and looked at him, but quickly shifted his eyes away.

"Well, Roger, with all due respect, you're not a lawyer. I think the city better check with counsel first, so we don't wind up in a suit brought by local businesses."

"I'll call our law firm tomorrow," said the mayor. "Maybe they'll say we can bring a nuisance suit or something." Most of the council nodded. Of course, by the time the mayor got a legal opinion the squatters would be long gone, and no one would worry about them again until next summer.

The rain ebbed and flowed but the weather did not change. Early the following afternoon Tigges found himself answering a complaint phoned in by one of the squatters from the airport manager's office. He drove down a narrow road located just above the high-tide line on the beach, though not beyond reach of the winter storms that soon would send sheets of ice crashing across the end of the runway. Gusts of wind and rain bucked the side of a muddy, rutted track, and he shifted into four-wheel drive.

He saw the fire down the beach, figures seated around it, and, as he got out, heard the murmur of voices carried on the wind. No laughter, just subdued talking—which cut off completely as they noticed Tigges.

The squatters camped in faded tents or under vinyl sheets spread over driftwood. They had a big blue plastic tarp set up next to the fire. The men stood up as he approached. Some had brought their families, women and children huddled around the fire. A woman sat in the entrance of one of the tents, holding a baby. Tigges stopped under the tarp, glad for anything that relieved the relentless pressure of the rain.

"They just came roaring in on their ATVs. Knocking over our tents, chasing people, scaring the hell out of our kids." The speaker was a big, redheaded, bearded man in his mid-thirties. He pointed out the tracks, not yet washed away. His face was flushed and Tigges smelled the booze.

"We've been coming here to fish for years," another man said. "We've got as much right as any Natives!"

Others cursed in assent. There wasn't much more to the story. No one had been hurt. Tigges promised to look into it.

"Sure you will!" the big man said, as Tigges walked back to the Blazer. "Just tell them if they come back, we'll be ready."

Tigges didn't need witness descriptions. He drove past the runway, the first shanties at the south of town, the hotel, and all the way to the dock on the north. There he turned away from shore, past vacant, flooded lots rutted by vehicles shortcutting the intersection. He slowed as he passed the Seal and Harpoon Bar. There were only two cars parked outside, so he didn't bother going in.

He found them coming out of the general store. Four boys in their teens or early twenties, led by Jimmy Tallman and his younger brother, whose name Tigges couldn't remember. Related—nephews or something—to the mayor. Tigges parked in front of their ATVS and got out.

"Heard you've been harassing the squatters."

Jimmy threw a leg over his ATV, leaned, and spit a thin stream of tobacco juice onto the ground. "Squatters?"

"Look, kid, just don't go riding down on the airport beach for awhile."

"This is Indian country, man." Jimmy's black eyes were expressionless. "We go where we want."

Suddenly, Tigges saw Jimmy lying on the ground, trying to raise his torso and coughing bright red froth. On his side, under one outflung arm, a hole the size of a golf ball blossomed blood, bits of lung tissue, and bone fragments from a rib. Bullet wound. Tigges held himself, careful to show no reaction until the vision passed.

"You want something else? Officer?" Jimmy was back on his seat, looking ready to spit again.

Tigges tried to find the right words. "You boys stay away from that squatter camp, or someone's liable to get hurt. If I find out you've been down there again, well, you're old enough to spend a night in jail."

But Tigges knew he couldn't stop it, and the futility must have shown on his face. As he turned back to the Blazer, Jimmy mumbled some remark at his back and the other boys laughed. Street punks, Tigges thought, they're the same everywhere. Usually just get what's coming to them anyway.

The ambulance hadn't been able to make it down the rutted track, but by then there was no reason to hurry. The .30-06 softpoint had taken him side to side, through both lungs. His ATV was stalled out against a partially flattened tent several feet away. Tigges and Henderson took photographs of the scene and witness statements from the squatters. Everyone had heard the shot, but no one admitted seeing anything. They wrapped Jimmy's body in a tarp and hauled it out to the waiting ambulance. The suspect was already secure in Tigges's jail.

Tigges and Henderson stood on the road as the ambulance left. The rain had subsided to a drizzle, although the low clouds still hid the horizon in every direction but seaward. The treeless tundra along the road showed a uniform dull brown, displaying none of the myriad colors of tiny flowers and turning leaves that would have been revealed in good daylight.

"I keep hoping for a break in the sky," Tigges said. "They say weather affects people's moods. If it doesn't let up there's liable to be more killing."

Henderson studied the seaward horizon. "Do you know the story about when the sky really did break open here? Funny, what you said just made it pop into my head."

Tigges shook his head and waited, nothing better to do than go back to the office and start his report.

"Long ago, before the whites came, the village once had a very hard winter," Henderson began. "Not much salmon in the fall, and they killed only a few seals all winter. By spring a lot of people had starved. One man, Nyluk, lost his whole family, and the ghosts of his wife, children, and parents haunted his house every night. He saw them but couldn't talk to them.

"One day Nyluk and another man went hunting seals in kayaks, past the ice offshore. They came to this place where the water was calm and the sky came down close, right overhead. Then they noticed the sky had broken open just above. Nyluk stood up, careful, in his kayak and put his head through the break in the sky. He saw a place that was warm and sunny, with flowers on the ground and bushes full of berries. Fish and game everywhere, just waiting to be caught. He tried to call to his friend, to tell him that the sky was better than living on the earth.

"But his friend couldn't hear him, and when he saw Nyluk disappear into the sky he paddled back to the village, fast as he could. The men all came back in their kayaks, but the sky was high above, not broken open like before. They found his kayak, but no sign of Nyluk. But then they found his body when they went back to the village, in his house. He had died that morning, before the hunt, but nobody knew it. Even Nyluk didn't know it. It was his ghost who went seal hunting. Ever since then, Nyluk is supposed to live in the sky, where he is always warm and is never hungry.

"My grandfather told me that when I was a boy." Charlie shrugged. "But people don't tell the old stories much anymore."

No one had ever told Tigges an Eskimo story. What if it's true, he thought. That the dead do go into the sky from here. He looked out at the Sound, wondering again who he had seen drifting there, up into the clouds. Not Jimmy Tallman, at least. Tigges had seen that boy dead like so many others, shot and lying in the mud.

Coming back by the airstrip, they passed two squatters, a man and woman, walking to town.

"That's his wife, with the baby," Henderson said. "And the other man who lives with them. His younger brother, I think. Must be going to see him in jail."

The squatter sat in the cell, staring at nothing until he heard Tigges and stood up. A tall, skinny blond man, with a beard and long hair pony-tailed in the back, like the hippies used to wear. Maybe news of the flower children just made it up here, Tigges thought. Or this is where they all went. Alaskan hippie, the kind who'll blow a man away for messing with his property.

"We need to fish to get us and the dogs through winter," the whiteman said. "That beach is the only place we got left." As if he actually believed he had been arrested for trespassing. Tigges couldn't recall seeing him in the camp before. He had given his residence as "twenty-four miles up the Noatak River."

"I just want to know about the shooting," Tigges said. He had read the man his Miranda rights at the time of arrest.

"I already told you, it was self-defense. Or defense of family. That's the same thing, ain't it?"

"Just tell me what happened."

The man's eyes narrowed, and he sat back down on the bunk. "No, I'm going to wait for my lawyer. I got that much right."

The public defender and assistant D.A. weren't due into town until Monday. Then maybe the judge would change the trial venue to Nome or Barrow.

Tigges could see Henderson holding the phone

and waving at him through the wire-reinforced office window.

"It's the mayor," Henderson told him, as he unlocked the door. "They're holding an emergency council meeting right now, and he wants to know if you can make it."

"Tell him I'm coming," Tigges said; and, after Henderson had hung up, "This'll probably last a while. Be sure and search his visitors when they get here."

"The baby too?" Henderson asked, in that same tone that Tigges could never tell was serious, mocking, or humorous.

Out in the pickup Tigges thought, certainly, damn it! The kid's blankets at least. He paused with his foot on the brake, then took it off. Hell, I can't babysit all the time.

The meeting produced nothing more than a protest letter to the state, holding the airport manager responsible for a human death and demanding that people not be allowed to camp on Native cultural sites.

"Margie Tallman's oldest boy gets shot right off his ATV, just for bumping into one of their tents, and we can't do anything else?" the mayor yelled.

"You can close the bars and liquor stores," Tigges said. But there was only more yelling and arguing, until the meeting finally broke up around nine o'clock.

The rain still streamed on Tigges's windshield.

This late it was just about dark, real night, the cloud banks closing off the last of the late-summer night's twilight. Back at the office he found that the squatter's visitors had already come, the brother now gone but the wife still sitting in the little one-couch lobby. She had red hair over green, wide-set eyes, a figure that looked too petite for living in tents and hauling fish into a boat, and a face that was probably pretty once, five or ten years ago when she married the squatter down in Oklahoma or Texas or wherever, before coming north to live in the bush. She rocked her baby, who was waking fitfully from a nap.

He could feel her eyes on his back all the way to the office, where Henderson was reading *Time*. The arrest report lay unfinished on the desk, and Tigges picked it up but couldn't give attention to the words. In the lobby the woman undid the buttons of her wool shirt to feed the baby. Tigges looked quickly over at Henderson, who happened to glance up from the magazine at the same time.

"Where'd the other one go? The brother?"

"Don't know," Henderson said. "Looked like he might want to get a drink. Maybe down to the 'Poon."

"Did you search him?"

"Yeah. He had him a knife."

"What happened to it?"

"Gave it back when he left."

"Goddamn it, Charlie! You give him back his knife and send him off to a bar?"

Charlie put down the magazine. "Well, we didn't

arrest him, and I didn't think we had any right to keep it. You like for us to go by the book."

"A good cop would find some excuse, at least until he left town. We can use police discretion to prevent violent situations." Tigges picked up his nightstick and took his rain parka from the coatrack. "I'd better get down there." He turned around and stopped.

He saw Charlie slumped sideways on ice-crusted gravel, mouth agape, pale with the frost that coated his face. Bottle in a brown paper bag clutched tightly to his chest. Oh, no, Charlie! Passed out drunk until you freeze—not that way! It made him mad, too mad to say anything aloud to his friend.

It was useless to say anything, anyway. He couldn't stand to look at Charlie like that, and went out, past the couch, not looking at the woman either but hearing the muffled sucking of the baby at her nipple. Before the door closed behind him the phone rang twice, until Henderson picked it up.

As Tigges drove down the street he noticed the wipers scraping on a dry windshield and turned them off. There were a lot of cars and ATVs in front of the bar this time of night. He pulled into a vacant space across the street and shut down the Blazer. The rain had finally stopped but the wind still slapped his parka in dying gusts coming up the street from shore. Across the Sound the sky seemed to be growing brighter, as if the bank of clouds were lifting there. A white couple walked quickly out of the bar, looked at him, and went on to their pickup.

He knew it had gone wrong as soon as he opened

the door because of the ring of silent faces around the bar. The bartender was on the phone, but watching the door. He pointed to the back of the room as soon as he saw Tigges.

Tigges pushed his way through the crowd to where the two men fought, panting on the floor, their legs kicking themselves around slowly in a circle as if they were a single wounded animal. They had wound up as unskilled or drunken fighters usually do, wrestling mostly, locked too close and flailing at each other's back. Left to themselves they could probably go on that way until exhausted without causing any real damage, so long as they didn't start biting.

Tigges grabbed the long hair of the Eskimo, hauled him up, and saw it was the other Tallman boy, who was maybe too young to have been in the place to begin with. "Get up," he said to the squatter. "You're both under arrest."

The Tallman boy spat something in Inupiaq, then, "Not in the same jail as him!"

The squatter got to his feet, still panting and shaking like an animal, a bloody smear under his nose. "All I done was come in for a beer and they jumped me. Don't a whiteman have any rights in this town?" He didn't look like he was out of his teens, either.

"Coming in here wasn't very smart after what your brother did," Tigges said. He started them both toward the door.

"I tried to tell them. The baby was in that tent!"

"That doesn't sound very smart either." Tigges

wasn't thinking about the conversation, but about getting them outside, where he could frisk and cuff them before anyone else got involved. They reached the door and Tigges pushed the Tallman boy out, his left hand still on the shoulder of the squatter beside him.

"It was raining, where was she supposed to put him, you dumb nigger!"

"*Tannik!*"

The second word came out of the crowd behind him in almost the same breath, a name he had heard before too, but only in this place and not with the old familiarity as the one uttered by the whiteman. A name that, ever since the first whaling ships had come out of the Bering Sea to this muddy spit of land, had been what they called the whites who had brought them drink and taken everything else. And Tigges, astonished to think it had been directed at him, turned to see who had spat out that word.

Turned into the blade so that it pierced his back just above the belt, the white boy's fist around the knife handle slapping his parka, the force of the blow and his own convulsive jerk propelling him through the door in a long, long fall.

He had never felt anything like the unbelievable, paralyzing pain, so strong it wouldn't let him cry out. He saw his hand lying next to his face but couldn't move it to get up. He heard the faraway sound of feet scattering stones in both directions on the street. He hadn't felt his face hit the gravel parking lot, he only knew he was lying there when he tried to breathe and took in a mouthful of muddy water. He struggled, managed a convulsion that turned him further onto his side.

Must have taken it right in the kidney, he thought. The pain began to spread into a numbness radiating from his back. He saw the shrinking form of the Tall-man boy under the streetlights, running toward shore.

Wonder where he expects to hide? No sooner had the thought come than Tigges was up and following, moving smoothly along the street. A light seemed to go with him, illuminating the houses and buildings he passed. There was no pain at all anymore; Tigges felt fine. He saw the boy disappear into one of the little shanties a block from the beach.

Why did he go in there? As Tigges thought it he moved toward the house and went inside; he wasn't sure how, since he didn't use the door. The boy was yelling in Inupiaq and shaking a woman asleep on a couch, beside a near-empty whiskey bottle. His mother?

The woman awoke and said, "Jimmy?" then looked at her other son, alive, and started crying, eyes screwed tight and the big tears squeezing out and falling with soft popping sounds, as if they were little bird eggs breaking on the peeling linoleum floor.

An older woman came out of a back bedroom. The boy started to speak but the old woman saw Tigges and let out a scream. The boy looked and he and both women started yelling and screaming. Tigges left quickly.

I shouldn't have just walked into their house, he

thought. Wonder where the other one's going? As he thought this, he was moving the other way along the street. Could see better higher up—and he floated up. He knew he ought to feel strange about that, but didn't. He spotted the white boy running toward the airport beach, where his boat was anchored. As if he could hide twenty-four miles up the Noatak.

Tigges felt he could go anywhere, felt he was going to go somewhere, knew the need to move on. But there seemed to be something he hadn't done yet. He wondered what was happening back at the bar, and found himself going that way, the wash of light flowing ahead of him. When he got there he heard a familiar voice yelling.

"Don't stare at him! Get out of here, shut that door!" It was Charlie. Now Tigges knew it had something to do with Charlie, what he had to do. The other people went back inside the bar and Charlie knelt down beside a dark form lying in front of the door, holding it, rocking and moaning, "My fault, my fault."

Tigges moved closer to see, but Charlie noticed the light and looked up first, right at him. Charlie straightened, and Tigges saw the body's face was his own.

"I'm sorry I got you killed, Roger," Charlie said. "I should have taken his knife, like you said."

Tigges tried to tell him no, but couldn't. He tried again, but couldn't make a sound.

"It's my fault, just like with my brother!"

Tigges saw his own body and moved toward it. It was still warm, and he found his way back inside.

His vision was very fuzzy, looking up at Charlie's face under the front door light. He couldn't feel anything in his hands or feet or anywhere. He concentrated on his mouth, tried to move it. His tongue felt thick and numb.

"N-n-n-n-no," he finally managed. His vision cleared as he gained his voice. "You warned . . . about knife. I screwed up, big time. Got careless, that's all."

A siren opened up in the distance, erupting out of the hospital garage at the other end of town. "Hang in there, Roger," Charlie told him. "Paramedics'll be here in a minute."

"Had to . . . tell you. Not your fault." Tigges looked directly at him . . . and saw Charlie a lot older, gray hair, slightly stooped—still here in the village, right here, looking down at this spot of ground. Then Tigges at last let his eyes roll away.

Head lying cradled in Charlie's lap, looking down the street toward shore, Tigges saw the bright patch of sky where the clouds were breaking apart to the northwest, and thought he saw all the way to the long, lightening hills across the Sound, their color already turning with fall, the tundra red and gold.

"Charlie?" he whispered; but then his voice failed. He wanted to ask the name of the story about the broken sky.

"Karuk," Henderson said. "My name is Karuk."

Tigges tried again to speak but it was too late. Because looking across the water called him away from his body again. Without looking back at his friend or even the emptiness of his own face, he floated down the street in a wave of light that illuminated the shanties, all the ones he knew and ones he had never noticed before, past where the land merged into the sea, rising slowly over the waves chopping parallel to shore, across the dark silty waters of the Sound, and up into the breaking August sky that only the Eskimos could name.

CHEECHAKO

Dana Stabenow

1

For many people today, the entire story of the Klondike Gold Rush is evoked by a single scene.

—Pierre Berton, *The Klondike Fever*

Their overcoats steamed in the red-hot glow of the tiny stove, the steam rising to form ice on the ceiling of the cramped canvas tent. After a day's slogging up and down the pass, they were each man and woman among them soaked to the skin, but it was so cold no one was willing to remove so much as a single layer of clothing. Frosted lashes and brows began to thaw, forming rivulets on cheeks that could be mistaken for tears, but the truth was they were too exhausted to weep. They sat instead in a silent circle, nine of them shoulder to shoulder, and thrust their hands and faces forward into the heat radiating from the stove like repentant sinners reaching for the light from above. If Jesus Himself had appeared before them, they would not have turned from the stove to greet Him, not even Isaiah Rowan. Rowan sat with his elbows on his knees, hands dangling between, his head bent, his eyes closed. His coat, made of moose-hide, had stood the day better than their thick woolen overcoats, but even that was dark with melted snow and sweat, and it smelled of urine and wood smoke.

But then they all smelled.

They had been strangers only weeks before, arriving separately in Dyea to begin the long trek over the Chilkoot Trail to the gold fields of the Klondike. In normal society Outside, only Lilly Lang and Jesse Cole might have met on business. The rest of them were from such different parts of the country and such disparate social strata that it was highly unlikely they would ever have come into contact.

Of necessity, they were now allies.

Slowly, the tent warmed to where the shedding of one's outer clothing seemed if not desirable then at least possible. Jesse Cole moved first, a long, rangy figure who seemed built of wire and nerve, a wide-brimmed hat casting a shadow over a hawk nose and deep-set eyes. He hadn't shaved since his first day in Sheep Camp and his face was bristly with a beard in which a few sprinkles of gray showed. He wore a duster, a long canvas coat that stopped just short of his ankles, revealing high-heeled leather boots more appropriate to riding than to climbing. There were marks where the boots had worn spurs. He doffed hat and coat and began to unpack pots and pans and utensils. He set a large, black kettle on the surface of the tiny stove and opened a flap of the tent just wide enough to reach through it and began to bring in frying pans full of snow, dumping them in the kettle.

Bertha DaFoe, her bulk so wrapped in multicolored scarves that it was hard to tell where they left off and her face began, stirred once, as if to rise and help him. Cole pressed her shoulder briefly with one hand and she subsided back onto the bound pack that served as her chair. The rest of them hunched against the cold air coming in through the open tent flap as if they were ducking a blow.

When enough snow had melted to fill the kettle halfway, Cole assembled a collection of tin cups and made coffee. He sugared it well and forced the cups into unresponsive hands, in some cases forcing cups to mouths. Slowly, one at a time, the group began to revive.

"I say," said Wilson Moore, the slender, dark-haired man with the white skin and the large blue eyes. "I say. That was a bit of a rough go. Stevens. I say, Stevens." He nudged the portly man next to him, asleep with his head on Moore's shoulder.

Stevens opened his eyes, blinked several times, and jerked upright. "I'm terribly sorry, sir."

"Think nothing of it, man. Perhaps you might, er—"

"Of course, sir. At once." Somewhat stiffly, Stevens got to his feet and stood looking about him for a moment, an almost comically bewildered expression on his face.

"The pack's just outside, Stevens," Moore said, and Stevens pulled himself together.

"Of course, sir." He paused with his hand on the flap, clearly reluctant to go outside.

"Hurry it up, man."

Stevens's shoulders stiffened. "Certainly, sir."

"Whyn't you get your own damn pack," said Billy Slavin, a thin boy of perhaps fifteen, his cheeks flushed with frostbite, his tone without any particular emphasis.

Moore stared down his nose at the boy. "Stevens is employed to get my, er, damn pack for me, Mister Slavin."

The boy, freckles standing out clearly on a broad white face, large-knuckled hands he had yet to grow into hanging awkwardly at his sides, ignored Moore's answer to look at the woman sitting next to him.

The second woman in the group, a slender sylph wrapped in white although somewhat bedraggled fur, put a slender hand on the boy's arm. He looked down at it and blushed on top of his freckles and frostbite. She smiled at him and patted his arm. She looked across at Moore, who raised an eyebrow. She smiled at him, too. The combined effect of bright red hair, brilliant green eyes, and full red lips over perfect white teeth was dazzling.

Frank Linville, sitting on her other side, cleared his throat and began to unbutton his coat with fingers that were still stiff from the cold. His face was large and coarse-grained, with a bulbous, red-veined nose, eyebrows like wiry-haired shelves, and small dark eyes set like raisins in bread dough. "Faith of our fathers, I don't want to be making that climb again anytime soon. "Down the Yukon for me, it is, after I'll be making my poke in the Klondike."

Lilly Lang's third smile was all his.

"Any chance of breaking out that portable bar of yours, Linville, and sharing out a wee drop of whiskey?"

Linville considered. "There might be, a fair chance," he said, cautiously.

"Then break it out, man, break it out." Linville hauled a large, wooden trunk forward and Moore watched him open the lid with a gaze that did not quite manage to conceal the hunger in it.

Linville measured out tots and passed them around in heavy shot glasses. Billy Slavin choked and wheezed on his, tears starting to his eyes. Lilly Lang sipped at hers with her wrist turned as if she held a teacup made of the finest china. Wilson Moore gulped his down in one swallow. So did Jesse Cole, but there was less desperation in his manner as he did so. Stevens said, "I have taken the pledge, sir," and Bertha DaFoe shook her head. Linville didn't offer Isaiah Rowan a drink, and Isaiah Rowan didn't ask. John Clancy appeared to be sleeping.

Bertha DaFoe stood up to remove her scarves and coat, revealing a sturdy figure that would have made two of Lilly's. Her hair was brown with the curls tucked into a neat bun at the back of her head, or at least it had been neat that morning. Her complexion was pale, although she had suffered cruelly from sunburn the one day during their trek that the clouds had parted, and her skin was still peeling five days later. Her eyes were an ordinary brown. She would have been unremarkable in any company. In this one, Lilly rendered her virtually invisible. The men didn't even look around when she moved to find the flour.

Cole began slicing bacon into a second frying pan on the stove. At that, even John Clancy began to wake up. He yawned hugely, jaws cracking with the strain, providing anyone who cared to look with an excellent view of a mouthful of brown teeth with significant gaps between them. Clancy was a man small in stature, with sparse black hair, a yellow look to his skin and quick, furtive eyes, a dark, vivid blue in color, his best feature. Lilly's smile to him was perfunctory.

"By god, that smells of heaven," Clancy said.

"The rest of you might break out the dishes," Cole suggested, only it wasn't a suggestion. His voice, low, slow, and deep, was a voice used to being obeyed, with the barest hint of threat, barely leashed, to back it up.

The smile that Lilly Lang bent on Jesse Cole was glorious, and even Wilson Moore, past connoisseur of the finer females life had to offer, sighed a little at the sight. Cole himself didn't seem to notice. He turned out the bacon and Bertha patted the dough into the bacon grease and put on the heavy lid. A few minutes later all was ready and the nine of them ate in hungry silence.

Bertha started to collect the plates.

Cole stopped her with a hand. "No. Someone else take a turn."

Francis Linville heaved himself to his feet and
nudged John Clancy with his toe. "Come on, boyo,
they've fed us well." He hauled John up by one hand
and the two men took the dirty dishes and pans outside to scour them clean in the snow. Isaiah Rowan,
short, stocky, brown of skin, hair, and eye, yet to say
a word, stowed the flour and bacon and brought
back the bedrolls beaten free of snow. Cole brewed
more coffee and had mugs ready when Clancy and
Linville reentered the tent. They sat drinking in silence for a few moments.

"Well," Francis Linville said. "That's that, then."
He looked around the circle. "Do you think he . . ."

Cole raised his head, free of its hat by now, which
made the expression on his face that much more
intimidating.

There was a brief silence. Linville cleared his throat
and said, "We made it, by god we did."

Billy Slavin's cheeks had returned to their normal
color. "Thirty-one trips I made. Thirty-one times I
climbed that—" He looked at Lilly. "Pass." At fifteen, he would have been forgiven the boast, but his
voice was too full of wonder and awe at the accom-
plishment for anyone to take offense.

"Thirty-six for me," Linville said cheerfully, checking to see that his liquor cabinet was locked.

Wilson Moore tried not to watch him doing it, and
said, "A strenuous trip, certainly. And not one I
would care to repeat."

"What's a dude like you doing on the road to the
Yukon?" Linville said, shoving the trunk in back of

him with one large paw. Bottles clinked and then were still. "What did you say you did?"

"I didn't say, Mr. Linville, but as it happens, I'm an architect."

"A what?" Billy Slavin said.

"An architect. I design buildings." Billy looked mystified. "Where are you from, Billy?"

"San Francisco," Billy said. "Born and bred. Ain't many in California can say the same."

"No, indeed," Moore murmured. "Well, do you know the Kipling Building on Broad Street?"

" 'Course I do. Everybody's knows the Kipling Building. They call it the Stairs back home. Some say it's short for 'the stairs to heaven.' Tallest building west of the Rockies."

Wilson paused. "Do they really?"

"Sure do."

"I didn't know that. Well, I drew the pictures that they built the Kipling Building from."

"Go on. Is that the truth?"

"It is. It's how I make my living."

"And so I put it to you again, Mr. Moore," Linville said, holding his mug out for a refill, "how is it you come to be climbing the Klondike with the rest of the scaff and raff?"

" 'Scaff and raff?' " Lilly said, stiffening.

"Sure and it's only a figure of speech, Lilly me darling," Linville said soothingly, patting her knee. Her smile less radiant, she moved her knee out of reach. Linville turned back to Moore. "It's obvious you come from money, Mr. Moore." He grinned at

Stevens, who remained impassive. "Sure and there's got to be an easier way to earn it than climbing that bastard out there. Forgive me, ladies."

Bertha was tucked into a dark corner in a pile of blankets arranged for her by Cole, her face a white blur. When she spoke her voice was a surprise, low, sweet, utterly feminine. "You know, Mr. Linville, we agreed in Dyea that no questions would be asked of those who did not care to answer."

Linville managed a courtly bow from his sitting position. "It's the right of it that you have, Miss DaFoe, ma'am, and I beg your pardon. And yours, Mr. Moore."

"No offense taken, Mr. Linville. It is natural we should be curious about one another. And there has been more climbing than getting acquainted over the last ten days. I don't mind giving you your answer, if you will satisfy my curiosity on a matter that has intrigued me from our first meeting."

Linville made an expansive gesture. "By all means, Mr. Moore, ask away."

"Where on earth did you find that extraordinary piece of luggage?"

"This?" Linville patted the wooden trunk in back of him and laughed. "That was hand-crafted for me in Seattle, to my own specifications. I'm a spirits salesman, see, and I was plying me trade from the farmers in Roy to the fishermen in Anacortes when the *Portland* docked in Elliot Bay. I looked at the size of the nuggets those boyos were using to buy eggs, and I said to meself, Frank me boy, it's the Klondike for you. Ah, thank you, Mr. Cole." He drank from his tin cup. "But I never had a liking to get my hands dirty, you see, so I thought I might bring my profession north. And then I heard tell of the thousands of men climbing that bastard out there—sorry, ladies—and how thirsty they might be at the top of it."

"Pretty thirsty," Moore said, fascinated, and even Cole was listening with the ghost of a smile.

"I know a woodworker in Seattle, and he built me this bar. You'll have noticed the legs that fold out so it can stand up on its own, the separate compartments for the bottles and the glasses. A fine piece of work it is, and well worth the money I laid out for it. I don't think I lost one bottle to breakage all the way from Seattle. That bastard out there—my apologies again, ladies, I'm afraid the Chilkoot Pass encourages strong language—accounted for two, but let that be. I sold whiskey for twenty-five cents a shot in Canyon City, for fifty cents a shot at Sheep Camp, for seventy-five cents a shot on the Stairs, and I plan to sell the rest of it for a dollar a shot at Lake Bennett. Building boats puts a powerful thirst on a man."

"My god, man," Moore said, for a change staring at Linville instead of his portable bar. "You must have made a fortune."

"Ah, well. One man's fortune is another's pocket change." Linville drank coffee, bright raisin eyes gleaming over the rim of his tin cup. "And you promised me a story of your own, sir."

Moore's eyes fell. A little behind him, his man, Stevens, sat still and stoic. "Unfortunately, Mr. Linville, it is not as interesting as yours. I am an architect, as I said before. I was working in San Francisco when the *Excelsior* docked. The story of the gold strikes along the Yukon stirred me to answer the call to adventure." His eyes, which had once again wandered to Linville's portable bar, pulled themselves away with an effort, to encounter Cole's measuring gaze. To do him credit, he didn't blush, merely firmed his mouth and raised his eyebrow in a question. Cole held his gaze for a long moment, and then nodded. Assent or approval, or both, no one could have said for sure.

"Miss Lilly?" Moore said. "May we have your story?"

Lilly Lang laughed. "You saw me playing my banjo in Skagway, Mr. Moore, and again in Dyea. I plan to play my way to the Klondike and give concerts in Dawson City. I expect to make my fortune before the year is out."

She had played to them one evening, her husky voice lifting them all out of fatigue-induced melancholy. No one doubted that she would accomplish her goal. Billy Slavin gazed at her with worshipful adoration.

"And you, boy," Linville said, "what brings you out on this godawful trail?"

Billy's face pinkened as all attention turned to him. "Well, sir," he said, Adam's apple bobbing nervously in his too-long, too-thin neck, "well, sir, I was a newsboy in San Franciso." He nodded at Moore. "I was at the wharf when the *Excelsior* docked, and those men were so hungry for news I could have charged them a dollar a paper and they would have paid it. I got to thinking, then. I got to thinking maybe I could sell a lot of newspapers to the miners who hadn't made the boat, to the miners still in the Klondike."

"That's what's in that big bundle?"

"Yes, sir, it is."

Linville clapped him on the back. "By god, that's some sharp thinking, Billy me boy. You'll clean up in Dawson, you will." He rubbed his chin. "You might want to rent them to customers, now, instead of selling them outright. Why deprive yourself of income by depleting your stock?"

"I hadn't thought of it, sir."

"Well, think of it, boyo!" Linville's eye lighted on Clancy. "And you, Mr. Clancy? Are you come north in search of the gold, then?"

"I am, Mr. Linville. But like you, I have no intention of pulling the stuff out of the ground myself."

"Have you not?"

"No. At home, I am an apothecary, and I, like you and young Billy here, have something for sale."

"And that might be?"

Clancy beamed. "Mosquito lotion."

"I beg your pardon?" Even Cole looked up.

"I have packed ten thousand bottles of mosquito lotion in my baggage, Mr. Linville, which I intend to sell to miners fighting the vicious, bloodthirsty creatures during the summer months. They're bad on the Klondike, they are." Clancy beamed with pride. "Oh, I've done my research, Mr. Linville, and there will come a time when we will all be grateful for the snow, indeed there will."

"I don't doubt you, Mr. Clancy, indeed I don't,"

Linville said. He looked at Cole, and even in the flickering light of the oil lanterns his expression was plain to read. Should he or shouldn't he?

Cole forestalled his decision by rising to his feet. "We've got a pile of supplies out there. We'll need to rise early to get the Mounties to count them off."

Bedrolls were rolled out forthwith, and occupied. They tossed for the spare to use as a pillow, and Frank Linville won. He gave it to Lilly Lang, a generous gesture rewarded by another blissful smile. Cole extinguished the last lamp, and left the last tallow dip to sputter out on its own.

The radiant heat of the stove lulled them all to sleep.

2

The greatest crime on the Dyea Trail that winter, as on all the trails, was not murder but theft.
—Pierre Berton, *The Klondike Fever*

It snowed two feet during the night. An incontinent bladder had Inspector James Blade of the North West Mounted Police first up, and so stuck with shoveling the snow away from the door of the tiny hut perched on the edge of the Chilkoot Pass.

"That'll larn you, Jamie," a voice mumbled from beneath a mound of blankets across the room.

What it would larn him was not specified. He stamped and swore his way into his boots and took hold of the shovel leaning against the wall. The door was reluctant to open, and he had to shovel a new path to the latrine. The path already had walls of snow too tall for him to see over.

It was a raw day, with the cold striking him to the marrow and the sky hanging over him like a lead weight. The brass buttons on his buffalo coat gleamed dully, and his breath left a trail of puffy white clouds hanging behind him in the air like little ghosts.

Like many of the Mounties hired by Superintendent Samuel Benton Steele, he was young, just twenty-one. The second son of an impoverished British nobleman, he had emigrated to Canada to seek his fortune and had found a measure of it in service to the law. He liked the country, the wide-open spaces, the towering mountains, even the loneliness of it, the miles and miles where no other human being had trod. He liked the few people who lived there, the Tlingit and the Athabascan, one of whose ancestral trade routes the Chilkoot Trail followed to the Klondike. Stalwart, hardy, spare of word, swift in action, generous with aid to those they deemed worthy of it, he felt at home among them, here in the great unknown.

Everyone laughed at him, of course, the rest of the detachment finding it amusing that anyone not born to it would actually consider living in this wilderness. "No saloons, no women?" Pierre Harkness said in dismay. "Jamie, Jamie, when the last stampeder has slogged his way up the mountain and the last white man has disappeared down the Yukon River, it'll be more than time to be moving on. Listen to your father, lad, and go home."

Blade didn't think he would want to go home, in spite of his father's importuning letters. In the meantime, he did his business in the latrine and went back to the cabin, to find Harkness had built up the fire in the small stove, had made coffee, and was now frying bacon. "You're not as useless as you appear then, Perry my lad," he said, stamping the snow from his feet.

Perry grinned up at him from where he sat as close to the stove as possible without actually setting himself on fire, his coat draped over his shoulders.

They were like enough to be brothers, both tall, fair-skinned, with light brown hair and dark brown eyes. Their shoulders were broad and a useful amount of muscle encased their limbs. They looked as if they could hold their own in a free-for-all, and indeed, if they couldn't have Samuel Benton Steele would have shown them the door.

They ate breakfast in silence. "Who's first out this morning, do you think?"

Blade blew on his coffee, considering. "If that fellow Jesse Cole has his way, his party will be on their way before noon." He glanced up at the roof, imagining the sky beyond. "Snow or no snow."

Harkness nodded. "An interesting group. They met in Dyea for the first time, is that right?"

"That's what the Clancy fellow said. Said Cole had the idea that a group of ten working together would make better time than ten individuals going it alone. I have to say, I think he's right. They made the haul in record time, at any rate."

"Miss DaFoe's stove helped."

"It made the difference," Blade agreed. "I can't believe she hauled the coal with her, but it made all the difference in her having the tent and the stove and the coal. The other nine had shelter and something hot to eat and drink and a place to warm up along the trail every day. And look at them now." He gestured over his shoulder. "Camped out on the summit, where no one but us have camped before, right in the middle of their piles of supplies for shelter."

"Probably snugger than we are. Especially with those two women in the group."

"You've got women on the brain, Perry," Blade said, but then didn't he have his eye on Isaiah Rowan's oldest daughter, Irene, she of the shining dark hair and flashing brown eyes, waiting, or so she said, for his duty to take him back to her? It was marriage he had on his mind, although his father and hers both would be horrified at the thought. They would have to run for it, he thought, considering the matter dispassionately. Yes. They would marry on the Canadian side of the border, and settle there, too, if her father proved intransigent, although Isaiah seemed a reasonable sort of man. She was an American and he was British, she was a Tlingit and he was British, but the New World seemed open to these kinds of possibilities.

He felt a little light-headed, and very, very happy, and went to his work with a song in his heart.

"Flour?"
"Four thousand pounds."

"Cornmeal?"

"Five hundred pounds."

"Beans? Beans?"

"I don't see them. I know we brought them, I think I carried the whole five hundred pounds up myself." Cole's voice was rueful.

In spite of what he knew about the man's past, Blade couldn't help but smile. "Not a thing to forget, I wouldn't imagine."

"No." Cole smiled back, and it was amazing how it changed his face, lighting it with intelligence and humor.

"Here they are, Inspector." Miss DaFoe, her substantial self wrapped in voluminous shawls and scarves, trod with an oddly light step over the snow to a mound of supplies.

"Thank you, miss." The light increased as the mound of supplies grew, oatmeal and rice and candles and bacon and yeast cakes and ginger and mustard and evaporated apples and coffee and condensed milk and laundry soap and matches and frying pans and shovels and axes and buckets and gold pans and rope and oakum and tents, a ton of goods for every stampeder who crossed over the Chilkoot Pass from the United States into Canada. Samuel Benton Steele had decreed it, that every single person who crossed the Pass must each have with them enough supplies to support themselves for one year. It amounted to about a ton of goods, and Blade was heartily sick of standing in snow up to his ears with more falling down his collar as he ticked items off a list. "That's it, then," he said at last with a sigh. "Your party is officially welcome into Canada, Mr. Cole."

"I thank you, Inspector Blade."

A small, gloved hand slipped into Cole's arm. "I thank you, too, Inspector," Lilly Lang said. "May I play you a song before we go?"

"Thank you for the thought, miss," Blade said, "but I'm afraid it would be wasted on me. I'm tone deaf."

Her smile dimmed for a moment. "I'm so sorry, Inspector."

He inclined his head, and after a moment, when Cole neither asked after her needs or moved to escort her elsewhere, she slipped her hand free and moved off, grace in the sway of her hips, not to mention invitation. Oh yes, she would do well in the dance halls of Dawson, would Ms. Lilly Lang.

Cole looked over Blade's shoulder. "Mr. Rowan."

Blade felt his spine straighten instinctively, and turned to meet the dark brown eyes of the man he hoped to make his father-in-law. "Mr. Rowan."

"Inspector Blade."

"Are you traveling on with Mr. Cole and his party?"

"I am, sir."

"I wish you a good journey, then."

"I thank you."

Blade stood as the group donned packs, and proceeded down the narrow trail that led to Lake Bennett. Linville was in the lead, his portable bar towed by a leather strap, packing down the snow for those to follow. Wilson Moore and his man, Stevens, were second, followed by John Clancy and the boy, Billy Slavin. The two women were next, Bertha DaFoe sturdy in her wrappings, Lilly Lang managing to remain slender in hers.

"Wait a minute," Blade said suddenly.

Cole and Rowan, hatted and coated and booted and bundled and about to swing into line, paused.

"There are only nine of you. Where is Doubilet?"

3

There was hardship on the trail, certainly, but comparatively few deaths and, considering the circumstances, little major crime.
　　　　—Pierre Berton, *The Klondike Fever*

"Absent a body with the clear mark of foul play upon it, I don't see what we can do," Harkness said somberly.

Blade didn't, either. He wished Superintendent Steele was here at the Pass, instead of on his circuit to Dawson City.

It was night again, and the long line of lock-steppers had retired to Sheep Camp, leaving the two Mounties alone on the edge of the abyss with nine people who were most probably murderers.

"Why are you so sure they killed him?"

Blade ticked his reasons off on his fingers. "One. He was part of the group ferrying supplies up the pass. Two. When we counted the supplies, there was enough for ten. Three. Only nine people are heading to Bennett. Four. They have offered no explanation of his absence."

They were silent for a few moments. The ice frozen to the inside of the roof dripped slowly into pans as the hut warmed from the little stove's fire.

"I didn't have as much to do with them as you did," Harkness said. "Who are the nine, and who is, or was the one?"

It was warm enough now to remove gloves and hat. Blade leaned forward to stir the beans in the Dutch oven. "Jean Doubilet was a Frenchman. I know little of the man, but to hear that group tell it they know even less. He had the hands of a laboring man, and his dialect was not that of Paris." He reflected. "He seemed to me to be more cunning than intelligent. He had shoulders like a lumberjack, and eyes quick to take the measure of a man and act accordingly. I would not have trusted him out of my sight." He paused, and added in deliberate tones, "I would not have thought him a man of whom it was easy to get the drop."

"And the nine remaining in the group?"

They were both thinking of the same man. "First and foremost is Jesse Cole."

"Why do I feel I should know the name?"

"You probably remember seeing it in one of the circulars the superintendent has received from officials in the States. Cole's a gunfighter out of Arizona. He's said to have killed eight men."

Harkness pursed his lips together in a silent whistle. "He's the leader?"

"Leader?" Blade considered this. "He's their surety,

perhaps, chosen to see that Smith's gang doesn't interfere with them, but I don't think they've got a leader."

"A democratic bunch of murderers," Harkness suggested.

"If he fought in the Indian wars and the cattle wars afterward, as is reputed, it is to be supposed he would have some tactical experience." Blade reflected. "One of their party was stationed at all times at the summit, guarding and marking their supplies. Miss DaFoe was set up at the halfway point to dispense refreshments and give the party a chance to warm themselves on their way up. It does smack of organization, but as to whether Cole's hand is behind it, I have no idea."

"And the others?"

"Francis Linville is a liquor salesman."

"Oh yes, I remember, the one with the portable bar."

"Yes. I will say this, he paid his excise tax without whining."

"Which only means he made a hundred times that on his way up the Pass."

"John Clancy is an apothecary, as I understand it, bringing a mosquito lotion of his own devising to sell to the people of the Klondike."

Harkness looked up and said quickly, "Does it work?"

"I don't know, but it ought to fetch twice its weight in gold in Dawson, if he manages to get it that far. William Slavin, the boy they all call Billy is taking a bundle of *San Francisco Chronicles* to sell to the miners."

"These Americans," Harkness said, not without admiration. "It's almost as if they're born knowing how to make money."

"It is, isn't it?" Blade agreed. "Although if Billy Slavin makes any he will have earned it. I've seen his bundle. It weighs more than he does. Isaiah Rowan, you know."

"He's going with them to Dawson, you said."

"Yes."

"Any idea why? He normally confines his exertions to the Pass."

"It is not within the province of Her Majesty's government in any way to interfere with the movement of her indigenous subjects along traditional aboriginal trade routes," Blade said.

If he'd had something ready to hand, Harkness would have thrown it. "Yes, well, I can read the bloody regulation handbook as well as you can, Jamie. Why do you think he's going?"

"Another back to carry supplies, I imagine. I would hope they are paying him for his time."

Harkness snorted. "I'd bet my entirely negligible expectations on it. What about the women?"

"Lilly Lang has worked saloons from Denver to San Francisco to Seattle. She spent the summer and fall working at the Red Garter in Skagway, saving her money for the trip to Dawson City, as she tells it."

"What kind of 'work' are we talking about?" Harkness's voice was frankly salacious.

"She claims to play the banjo well. I haven't heard her. That would be enough, certainly, to earn a good living. The girls in Dawson are earning forty dollars a week for dancing alone, plus twenty-five cents for every drink they sell."

Harkness considered. "I might marry her, and let her make my fortune for me."

"You might," Blade agreed. "There might be those in her party who would be in line in front of you, however."

"Cole?"

"Not Cole. If I'm not mistaken his interest lies with the second woman."

Harkness was incredulous. "Bertha DaFoe? What does Cole see in her?"

Blade's Irene was a lush, plump armful herself, and he eyed Harkness coolly. "A good heart, and a sharp eye for commerce. She hauled a lit stove all the way up the Pass, along with enough coal to keep her party warm all the way to Bennett."

"What is her plan for the Klondike?" Harkness's brow furrowed, and added, "Do you notice, Jamie, that none of them are miners, or have any wish to be?"

"They will be mining the miners, Perry, as the saying goes. And, in the end, they will very probably go home with more money in the bank than do the miners themselves."

"What is Cole going to do? Wave that bloody great pistol of his about and frighten people out of their pokes?"

"He's a killer, not a thief." Blade thought of Cole's ability to command obedience with a look, and added thoughtfully, "He'd make a good marshal."

Harkness choked over his coffee, but he had to admit the truth of it.

They ate their bacon and beans in silence. Blade washed up, although it was a job to try to keep ahead of the mold growing on dish, bunk, clothes, and tent. "It's a dog's life," Harkness said sadly from a prone position on his bunk.

Blade brewed coffee in the clean pot, and they stirred in condensed milk and sweetened their tin cups heavily with sugar chipped out of a sack.

"What's to be done?" Harkness said.

It was snug in the little tent, with the fire crackling in the stove, and with almost all the ice melted from the ceiling, nearly dry. The silence outside was absolute, no noise coming through the falling snow from the other tent down the way.

"I'll talk to Cole in the morning," Blade said.

4

All winter long, from Sheep Camp to the summit,
for four weary miles the endless line of men
stretched up the slippery slope, a human garland
hanging from the summit and draped across
the expanse of the mountainside.
   —Pierre Berton, *The Klondike Fever*

Cole heard him out in silence the next morning with the snow falling around them. The light shone through it, as if the sun were determined on hammering its way through from the other side. They stood in silence when Blade finished, and in spite of his best efforts Blade knew there was an implied plea as he came to an end.

The rest of the party was bundling packs together, cinching them to packboards, helping each other strap into them. Frank Linville, big, bluff hearty fellow that he was, paid particular attention to Lilly Lang, and was rewarded with a radiant smile. Wilson Moore shrugged into his without fuss, and then aided his man, Stevens. "Really, sir—"

"Hush, man. You might injure yourself and then where would I be?"

Bertha DaFoe put her shoulders into the harness she had devised to pull the sled carrying her stove and its sacks of fuel. Flakes of snow hissed against the stove's sides and melted away into nothing. She looked up at Cole. Her smile was so bright it made Blade's eyes narrow. He saw an answering smile in Cole's eyes, quickly masked when he saw Blade watching.

Isaiah Rowan roped a pack twice the size of everyone else's to a packboard and shrugged into it as easily as one might shrug into a coat. He stood with the rest of them, waiting on Cole's signal to move out. Blade was impressed with their almost soldierly bearing. What had forged them into this disciplined, determined unit?

He looked again at Cole and found his answer.

As if Cole had been waiting for Blade to come to this point, he said, "I don't know what happened to Mr. Doubilet, Inspector Blade. I will say that he was an irritant to the group. He would, I believe, have proven an irritant to any group of which he was a member. I should never have permitted him to join us. It was my mistake, and my mistake alone." Cole hesitated. "His loss is my responsibility, and mine alone."

What did that mean? In an attempt to sting Cole into something approaching veracity, Blade said, "If spring comes and Mr. Doubilet is recovered, shall I have his body shipped to Dawson for burial?"

Cole's expression didn't change. "Certainly. I will be happy to bear the responsibility of his interment."

He waited a moment, to see if Blade had anything further to say. When Blade remained silent, Cole inclined his head. "All right," he said, his deep, authoritative voice carrying easily through the falling snow. "Let's move out."

Once more they set out along the trail. It wasn't Blade's last sight of them, as they would spend the next week ferrying their supplies from the summit of the Pass to the small city that had grown up overnight on the shore of Lake Bennett, where they would build their boats and float down the Yukon River to Dawson and fortune. They always had a pleasant word for him, and once he hiked down the trail to where Bertha DaFoe had stamped out a small resting place in the hollow of a cliff, there to set up her stove and dispense hot food and beverages to those members of her party. She was pleased to ladle him out a bowl of stew, which he was bound to own was perfectly delicious, and for which he thanked her sincerely, as it was another cold, snowy day on the Chilkoot Trail.

The last time he saw the party together was the

day they arrived to pick up the last of the goods they had stowed at the summit. Rowan was the last out. Blade came up as Rowan was shouldering his packboard. "Isaiah."

Isaiah nodded. "Inspector."

Impulsively, knowing it was wrong, thinking fearfully of his Irene, he said, "He ought at least to be buried, Isaiah."

Isaiah's face, square and brown and uncompromising, didn't change. Nor did he pretend ignorance. "He is buried." He looked at the falling snow, and then at Blade. A pause. "If he's dead."

"What did he do?" Blade said, daring greatly. "Did he, er, attempt to offer outrage to one of the women?"

Isaiah, settling the packboard on his shoulders, considered. "Not under my eye."

Which was no kind of answer. Blade, discovering with some surprise that he sought an excuse more than an explanation, said, "Did he slip and fall down the mountain? Was he lost in a snowdrift?"

Isaiah stared into the distance with expressionless brown eyes. "He was a sinner." The Presbyterians had done their work well among the Tlingit, and Isaiah Rowan knew a sinner when he saw one.

"Against which Commandment did Mr. Doubilet offend?"

A smile flitted across Isaiah's face, the first one Blade had ever seen. "Thou shalt not be a cheechako in the land of the Kolosh."

Before Blade could say anything else, Rowan set off, his figure soon to be lost in the drifting snow.

The sun rose and the long line of people began to lurch up the mountain once again. Blade checked off the supplies of one hopeful stampeder who was ready to follow the Cole party on to Lake Bennett. He was a German, with a fresh, open face, wide blue eyes, a massive frame with shoulders an ax handle wide and hands like an ape's. It had taken him thirty-two trips up the Golden Stairs and the Scales, half of it on his hands and knees, to haul his supplies to the top of the Pass, and on the return slides down the icy chute next to the trail had worn his woolen trousers down to his underwear. He was very young, Blade thought, forgetting that he was just twenty-one himself and as such three years the man's junior. "Flour."

The stampeder, armed with one of his two required shovels, rooted industriously in his pile. "Here, Inspector."

"All four hundred pounds?"

"All, sir. Here the sacks are."

And the sacks were there. Blade checked it off his list. "Sugar."

"Wait. No, is here. An hundret pounts."

"Coffee."

"Twenty-four pounts."

"Tea."

There was a slight delay and a few muffled curses in German before the five pounds of tea was resurrected. "Butter."

"Twenty-fife cans."

And so it went, from the thirty-six yeast cakes to the twenty-five pounds of evaporated peaches to the

fifteen pounds of salt, to the pick, handsaw, whip-
saw, buckets, gold pan, two frying pans, dishes, cut-
lery, the steel stove—

"Wait."

The stampeder—what was his name?—looked anxious. "The problem what? Here the stove is."

"Wait a moment, if you please," Blade said.

He turned and walked the few steps it took to
bring him to the edge of the precipice. It was high
noon, by his watch, and the snow had ceased falling
an hour before. The clouds still clustered thickly
about the mountains and threatened to close in again
as soon as their forces were gathered, but a narrow
strip of blue had opened over the Trail and the sun's
rays trickled through like a golden stream. For this
one moment Blade could see all the way back to
Dyea, and the entire unbroken line of human figures
distorted by the packs on their backs. The lucky wore
fur, the unlucky wool, but they would all be soaked
through with sweat and snow by the time they
reached the top of the Pass. What would they not
give, Blade thought, what would they not give for a
warm fire to warm their hands by and a hot drink
to warm their insides?

"Almost anything," he said out loud, earning a
nervous glance from the German anxiously waiting
behind them.

Of course, he thought. Of course. He burned with
shame that he had not seen it before.

The stove.

Doubilet had tried to take the stove, the thing that
had brought them together in the first place, the one

thing that the partnership hinged upon, the one thing that if it were stolen would have cast awry all their plans, could, in fact, have killed them.

It sounded like justifiable homicide to Blade. He'd tell Irene about it, the next time he was in Haines. He was sure she'd agree.

In the meantime, he turned back to the German. "A pick?" he said.

FINDING LOU
John Straley

It was early spring, sleet fell on old snow
and I needed to find a fisherman named Lou.
I'd heard he'd seen a bar fight almost a year ago
but he wasn't answering my calls so,
I walked to the swimming pool to sit in the bleachers
with a book I knew I wouldn't read
and watched dozens of slick-skinned children
slide back and forth, through the chlorinated water.

I found my only son, slippery and pink
rolling along in his lane as if he were a manatee,
dreaming through his warm, clean, world;
dreaming through the expanse of chlorinated water,
while on the other side of the walls
sleet glazed the town, and the icy mounds
of old snow were sinking down
revealing dog turds and discarded sandwich boxes
thrown down months ago.

Up in the hills brown bears were sleeping in their
   dens dreaming of slick fat
salmon, and starved down carcasses of snow-trapped
   deer.
But in the forced air of the junior high school
   building,
mothers and fathers sat in the bleachers watching,
some were laughing and others reading through
newsletters, or fumbling with stubs from checks
   they'd written.
I asked Norm if he'd seen Lou, and he shook his head
but said Lou might have been up to the bar around
   three o'clock.

I stepped through the steam
to hurry my son so we could walk down to the street.
He dresses quickly, my good luck. Ten years old and
   will still walk
with me in public but as I hold his hand crossing
   the street
he wiggles free and I feel the heat from the shower
   on his palm,
and smell the chlorine on his damp skin.
Hail fell, striking like frozen peas, and the street
became a frantic rubble of white, before turning to sleet.

I walked and thought of getting done with this case
and maybe looking at the short listings of State jobs.
My son was not speaking but walking beside me
dreaming those questioning dreams of his:
What does "inflammable" mean? Who is Demi Moore?

What happens when people die?
His mind ticking like a combine along the furrows
of the blue-black universe.

The barmaid asked what I wanted and I told her I
    wasn't drinking
then asked if she had seen Lou
and could I get some change for my kid
so he could play some games.
She said, "Don't let him get wild," and I said,
"Fuck you . . . get wild. This is my kind, Katie. Give
    me bourbon and water,"
and she did, then nodded to her left where Lou was
    sitting like
a broken fencepost at the bar.

All Lou could remember were some skippers push-
    ing and swearing,
someone spitting, and a couple of cheap shots to the
    rib cage.
When it moved out on the sidewalk Lou didn't fol-
    low, why should he?
The fight hadn't made much of an impression
for it wasn't until hours later, someone found the
    older guy
with his leg broken, his face split up the middle
lying down on the docks where no one was dancing
and the gulls were hee-hawing their laughter in the dark.

"Fights. Hell I've seen fights,"
Lou said, but he hadn't seen the blood
or the bone pushing up against the old man's pants leg,

and a year later, Lou was sitting here drinking, and
   laughing,
in the same bar where my son was shooting down
spaceships and Katie was talking to a regular
who could barely find his mouth with a cigarette.
I drank my drink and thought who was I kidding
   about getting a State job.

The cold rain fell all around the bar
while Lou was telling me how sorry he was,
and Katie leaned back to ask
if I wanted anything else and I said,
No I had to go home so I could get some sleep
and she said, "You'll have plenty of time for sleep
   when you're dead,"
then the regular bought me another drink,
while my son rattled and kacked at the alien ships.

This is how life goes:
We dream and cross each other's dreams like the
   ripples
some raindrops leave.
Sometimes we pay attention but often, not in time.
I sat and drank and forgot about Lou
or the State job, or the swimming pool.
I cashed a check while darkness crept like steam
   around the windows
and the rain kept slicing down . . .

Finally I had to go, so I called his mother to come
   get us,
and although she wasn't happy, she said she would.

Waiting there, I held my son's hand and I told him
   this:
"Up in the hills the bears are not really sleeping,
but they live in an uneasy torpor,
and I think this is the way God wants it
to protect his most dangerous mammals,
from killing one other."

Then he smiled at me sweetly
as if he could see the great blue planet
glittering like a raindrop falling through the dark
and he asked me for another quarter.

About the Authors

Donna Andrews is the award-winning author of four novels, including *Murder with Peacocks*. She is a member of Sisters in Crime, the Mystery Writers of America, and the D.C. Webwomen. A lifelong Virginia resident, she visited Alaska for the first (and she hopes not the last) time in 2001 for the Left Coast Crime mystery convention.

Michael Armstrong moved to Anchorage, Alaska, in 1979 and has lived in Homer, Alaska, since 1994. He is the author of four novels, including *After the Zap* and *AQVIQ,* and numerous short stories. Michael and his wife, Jenny, live in a cabin they built themselves in the hills 1,200 feet above Homer, which they share with a large cat and an even larger dog.

Mike Doogan was born and raised in Alaska. He lives in Anchorage, where he is a columnist for the

Anchorage Daily News. He is the author of two books of nonsense about Alaska, *How to Speak Alaskan* and *Fashion Means Your Fur Hat Is Dead,* and the editor of the essay collection *Our Alaska.*

Virgin Islands resident **Kate Grilley** is the award-winning author of the Kelly Ryan/St. Chris Caribbean short stories and the mystery novels *Death Dances to a Reggae Beat* and *Death Rides an Ill Wind.* During her second trip to Alaska, Kate saw a moose, rode on a dogsled, and attended the Miners and Trappers Ball.

An Alaska resident since 1974, **Sue Henry** lives and writes in Anchorage when she is not on research trips to gather settings and information for future books. She has written ten award-winning mysteries in her Jessie Arnold/Alex Jensen series and a number of short stories and articles. Her latest novel, *Cold Company,* recalls an actual Alaskan serial killer who flew his victims into the rugged Alaskan wilderness and was one of the first to be profiled by the FBI. The "stunning locales" of her mysteries "appeal to armchair travelers . . . as well as Henry's usual fans." *(Publishers Weekly)*

Anne Perry was born in Blackheath, London, in 1938. She enjoyed reading from an early age and two of her favorite authors were Lewis Carroll and Charles Kingsley. It has always been her desire to write, but it took Anne twenty years before she produced a book that was accepted for publication—*The Cater*

Street Hangman, which came out in 1979. Anne chose to write about the Victorian era by accident, but she is happy to stay with it because it was a remarkable time in British history, full of extremes, poverty and wealth, social change, expansion of empire, and challenging ideas. In all levels of society there were the good and the bad, the happy and the miserable.

Father **Brad Reynolds**, S. J., is author of the Mark Townsend mystery novels. His work as a writer and photographer has appeared in magazines and newspapers all over the nation, including *National Geographic*, *America* magazine, *American Scholar*, *The Seattle Times* and the *Anchorage Daily News*. He resides in Portland, and in Toksook Bay whenever he can.

Kim Rich is the author of the memoir *Johnny's Girl* (Alaska Northwest Books, 1999), which has been adapted to the stage and television. She has an M.F.A. in Creative Writing from Columbia University. Currently working as a screenwriter and novelist, Kim is a member of the writing faculty at Alaska Pacific University.

S. J. Rozan, author of the Lydia Chin/Bill Smith series, was born and raised in the Bronx. She has won the Shamus, Anthony, and Edgar awards. A New York City resident, Rozan is a practicing architect and a very bad basketball player.

James Sarafin is a lawyer who lives in Anchorage and visits Alaska whenever he can. "The Word for Breaking August Sky" first appeared in the July, 1995 issue of *Alfred Hitchcock Mystery Magazine*. Originally conceived as a dark fantasy, it won a ghost story contest sponsored by Nan A. Talese/Doubleday, and the Robert L. Fish Award (best first mystery story) from the Mystery Writers of America.

Dana Stabenow is the author of nineteen novels, including the Edgar Award–winning *A Cold Day for Murder*, and an explorer for *Alaska Magazine* Television. She hosts a radio book club of the air broadcast on Alaska public radio and writes a travel column for *Alaska Magazine*. She lives in Anchorage and can be reached through her Web site at www.stabenow.com.

John Straley is a private investigator and the author of the Cecil Younger series of Alaskan mysteries. His first book, *The Woman Who Married a Bear*, won the Shamus award for best first mystery in 1993. Straley has lived in Sitka, Alaska, for the last twenty-five years.

DANA STABENOW

"An accomplished writer... Stabenow places you right in this lonely, breathtaking country...so beautifully evoked it serves as another character." —*Publishers Weekly*

BETTER TO REST: *A Liam Campbell Mystery*
0-451-20702-5
Alaska state trooper Sergeant Liam Campbell is the representative of law and order in the fishing village of Newenham-yet struggles to keep his own life on an even keel. Now, just when his future is starting to heat up, he delves into a case of a downed WWII army plane found mysteriously frozen in a glacier.

NOTHING GOLD CAN STAY
0-451-20230-9
Shocked by a series of brutal, unexplainable murders, Alaska State Trooper Liam Campbell embarks on a desperate journey into the heart of the Alaskan Bush country-in search of the terrible, earth-shattering truth...

SO SURE OF DEATH
0-451-19944-8
Liam Campbell has lost more than most men lose in a lifetime: his wife and young son are dead; his budding career is in a deep freeze ever since five people died on his Anchorage watch. Demoted from sergeant to trooper, exiled to Newenham, a town teeming with fiercely independent Natives, he lives on a leaky gillnetter moored in Bristol Bay, brooding on how to put down roots on dry land again and rekindle his relationship with bush pilot Wyanet Chouinard, who won his heart long ago, and then broke it.

To Order Call: 1-800-788-6262